L. M. C.

CROMARTIE V. THE GOD SHIVA ACTING THROUGH THE GOVERNMENT OF INDIA

RUMER GODDEN

CROMARTIE V. THE GOD SHIVA ACTING THROUGH THE GOVERNMENT OF INDIA

MACMILLAN

First published 1997 by Macmillan

an imprint of Macmillan Publishers Ltd
25 Eccleston Place, London SW1W 9NF
and Basingstoke

Associated companies throughout the world

ISBN 0 333 71548 9

1 3 5 7 9 8 6 4 2

A CIP catalogue record for this book is available from
the British Library.

Typeset by SetSystems Ltd, Saffron Walden, Essex
Printed and bound in Great Britain
by Mackays of Chatham plc, Chatham, Kent

pp 84-5: 'Childhood' from *Poems 1906–1926*
by Rainer Maria Rilke, translated by J. B. Leishman.
Reprinted by permission of the Estate of the author and of Chatto & Windus.

LONDON

'CROMARTIE VERSUS the God Shiva. No, thank you,' said Sir George. 'Walter, I really don't think I can take this case.'

Sir George Fothergill, QC, was head of one of the most prestigious sets of chambers in London's Inns of Court. Walter Johnson was its head clerk.

The Chambers, though not in Lincoln's Inn, were nearby in Lincoln's Square. In the tall old house, Sir George and his deputy head of chambers, Miss Honor Wyatt, QC, had the two panelled first-floor rooms. The rest of the barristers in the set worked two or three together while Walter was in the spacious basement, which he liked because it opened on to the narrow terrace of garden. His 'snug', as he called it, not only had his desk, filing cabinets and shelves of law books on every wall, but his armchair by the fireplace – in winter the flickering gas fire was always lit – with a fine Persian hearth rug and above, on the mantelshelf, his collection of toby jugs. Next door was a large office for the deputy clerk – Walter's son, Johnny – Johnny's own assistant, Jeffrey, and his accounts clerk, Elizabeth. Ginevra, the perky young receptionist, had her desk with its telephones above in the front hall.

'It's always the head clerks who really run chambers,' Sir George would say. 'Walter's family have been in the set longer than any of us.'

'Yes,' Walter agreed. 'John Johnson my father, then me, Walter Johnson, and now Johnny, my son, who's only been here five years, and he's just had a baby son. Perhaps he ... I like continuity,' said Walter.

Now Sir George was going on: 'I don't want to oppose you, Walter – when have I ever?' he asked. 'But this is too fantastical – a Hindu god going to law.'

'Acting through the Government of India, sir, which seems solid enough to me.'

'It can't be solid if it's a spirit, which I don't believe is active. No, I can't bring myself to do it. We should be a laughing stock.'

'Ask Miss Wyatt what she thinks.' Walter was a diplomat.

—◆—

'A laughing stock? Why?' asked Honor Wyatt. 'I find it piquant.'

'*Piquant?*' Sir George was outraged.

'Yes. It seems to let in another air – a fresh one. It could become a sensation, which would extend us. And, George, think too of the fee.'

'Yes, indeed,' said Walter, and he was soon justified. When the Government of India heard rumours that Sir George Fothergill was hesitating, the fee was immediately doubled.

'It's a plum,' Honor said. 'We can't let it go. I wish I could take it.'

'*I* wish you could, Miss Wyatt, but you're on the Huntingdon case.'

The Huntingdon case was exciting wide and horrified interest. Lord Ian Huntingdon, eldest son of one of the country's oldest and richest aristocratic families, had learned he was to be disinherited for deceiving his father over the estate and an attempt would be made to strip him of his title, but before this could be implemented the old Marquess had been found dead. It might have been a heart attack but the 'young idiot', as Honor called him, had also killed his mother the Marchioness. Honor was briefed for the defence – and this case had brought a great deal of notoriety. 'There's nothing, except the royals, that can excite British public sensationalism more than the aristocracy,' she said regretfully. 'It may take weeks, even months. I wish I *were* free but I'm not.'

'Then who?' asked Sir George.

Walter knew he had to say what had been in his mind all along. 'Sir, I've been thinking of Mr Dean.'

That took Sir George by surprise. 'Young Michael?'

'He isn't all that young, sir, and doing remarkably

well. His handling of that awkward Gibbons case was masterly – if that's not too strong a word. Old Gibbons was so crafty he'd have defeated most of us. And it seems to fit, sir. Mr Dean was born and brought up in India.'

'Only until he went to school,' Sir George cavilled. 'As far as I know he hasn't been back.'

'No,' Honor intervened, 'but if you've been in a country as a child, it is, as it were, in your bones, and I think he's still attached.'

At thirty-one Michael Dean was the senior of all the junior barristers at 2 Lincoln's Square. There were sixteen of them and Michael had recently been made a Leading Junior, able to lead another barrister in a case – 'For which normally you need ten to fifteen years' call,' Honor had told his parents, 'unless you're exceptionally able and confident, which Michael is after only seven, and we would never hold back such talent.'

Honor knew his calibre: in his early days, when he had been a pupil, she had taken him for six months' training. To repay her he had done all her paperwork, as was customary in chambers, 'And learned and learned,' he often said, 'by grace and favour and luck.'

'Not luck,' said Honor. 'Brains, hard work and determination from the very beginning.' That was true. 'It's as difficult to get into a set of chambers like Sir George Fothergill's as it is to climb Everest without oxygen,' she would say. She knew: she had had to do it. 'And I had influence. Michael did it all himself. I've often wondered how he can afford it.' Every barrister in the set had to pay his or her own way: rent, services, telephone and fax, electricity. 'His parents couldn't help him much,' Honor told Sir George now. 'They're teachers, quite ordinary — except that his father is a teacher poet. Michael has poetry in him, too, so this case may not be at all a strange idea to him. Though he's astute, there's something undoubting in him — you would call it credulous.' She smiled. 'Why not call him in and talk to him?'

Sir George opened the proceedings. 'Michael, you have undoubtedly heard of the case concerning a Mr Cromartie and the Hindu god Shiva, acting through the Government of India.'

'Of course, Sir George. "Versus the God Shiva" — that's caught people's attention. The whole of Chambers is buzzing with it.'

'And that is just what I find too fantastical. The case has been offered to us but—'

'Sir George, you're not going to refuse it?' Michael was so alarmed that he forgot to whom he was speaking.

'I think I must. A Mr Bhatacharya has just come to see me from Delhi. He's a high-ranking official if not a minister.'

'He's a minister,' said Walter.

'Obviously he wants us — hasn't his own government chosen us? — but I confess I feel out of my depth. If it were a case of a valuable antique bought or stolen and taken to another country with the idea of selling it there for profit, of course I could understand and sympathize, but this! Candidly I'm afraid of it. We could be brought to ridicule.'

'I think it might enhance us,' Honor put in. 'Don't you see, George? The inclusion of the god makes the charge more serious.'

'Mr Dean, sir,' Walter was steering skilfully, 'you remember something of India, don't you? Wouldn't you agree with that?'

'Completely,' said Michael.

'Then can you tell us why?'

'Because in India the gods are alive, living as well as sacred, so anything to do with them is sacrosanct.'

'But to go to law!'

'Well, Indians can be fanatical – just like us,' Michael admitted. 'Of course, I don't know a great deal about India now, but I do know that most Hindus live their religion. To them it's not something apart as it so often is with us, but the core of every day, so much so that to us it is almost shockingly everyday. The Hindu gods eat and drink, fall in love, marry just like us. For Hindus sex, too, is sacred. The symbol for Shiva is the *lingam*, the phallus, the male generative organ, while, for the various manifestations of his goddesses, it is the *yoni*, the vagina.'

Sir George's expression showed that this was

distasteful to him, but Michael was so carried away that he had almost forgotten him. 'They're found in every Shiva temple. This bronze, I understand, is a little Nataraja Shiva, in his cosmic dance around the universe, extremely sacred. In India, to steal a Nataraja denigrates it, which is blasphemy.'

'Blasphemy!' Sir George was shocked.

'The worst crime of all, the only one that can't be forgiven,' and Honor quoted, '"He that shall blaspheme against the Holy Spirit hath never forgiveness." It is, to some extent, in every religion.'

'In India it's law,' said Michael. 'Oh, Sir George,' he was on fire, 'I do so hope you'll take this case.'

Sir George looked from one to the other. 'Cosmic dance. Sex. You'd better tell me who or what this Shiva is. How does he fit in?'

Michael did not answer at once. He won't hurry, not even for George, thought Honor, pleased. She always liked to look at Michael: not tall, he was slim, quick in his movements; dark-haired, he had hazel eyes, which were oddly penetrating when he was fighting in court, but they could light up with fun and laughter. Although she was his senior not only in rank but by several years, Honor liked going out with him. 'And he seems to enjoy it, not just politely – he really does.'

'Hasn't he got a girl of his own age?' Sir George had not meant to cast any slur on Honor, who was not at all perturbed.

'Dozens, I should think, but nothing serious. He seems adept at avoiding that.'

'Wise man.'

'No,' said Honor. 'He's clever but not wise – and he's so consistently steady in court that it's as if nothing touches him deeply. I think Michael has a lot to learn. Perhaps India will teach him.'

Now Michael began: 'Hinduism is an old, old religion, going back to the elemental gods – Surya, the sun, Indira, god of storm and rain, Agni, fire – and they still, in a way, remain. A good orthodox Hindu wife will hold a kitchen *puja* – prayer. It's a holy day when all the pots and pans are scoured, cleansed and tidied. The shelves are freshly papered, marigold garlands hung along them, vases of fresh flowers brought in. Finally a new fire is lit. Anyone can recognize the elements in that simple festival, but as the Hindus became more educated, less simple, they wanted something not as abstract as the elements, close but still powerful, and deeper than themselves, mystical, and so the individual gods manifested themselves.'

'It seems to me they have hundreds of gods,' said Honor.

'Only three. Most are aspects, male and female, of the great Hindu trinity: Brahma the Creator, "who has made all things visible and invisible", as Christians say, Vishnu the Preserver, who holds all things together, and Shiva the Destroyer who, because he brings death, is also resurrection. To Hindus, death is simply a stage in the cycle of creation, so Shiva in his dance around the world is god of all movement, especially in time and all life. That is why he is so often shown as a Nataraja – *nata* from dance, *raja* meaning king or royal, a great king against whom one must not trespass.' He paused. 'He must be deeply insulted now by being stolen, which is why the Government of India is so outraged.'

There was a silence until Sir George said, 'Thank you, Michael.'

When he had gone: 'I thought Michael got by on his charm. I didn't know he could speak like that.' Sir George blew his nose.

'He usually does, but that was the real Michael. George, let Walter give him the brief.'

'I had half a mind to when he was speaking, but we have to be careful. However fantastical, this is an important case and Michael is still a junior.'

'Senior Leading Junior,' Honor reminded him.

'But, still . . . will they accept him?'

'If they're told he's one of the most brilliant of the oncoming young barristers in London,' suggested Honor.

'Isn't that putting it rather high?'

'No,' said Walter, 'and he's greatly in demand. I could do with more Mr Deans.'

'Well, if you can't spare him to go to India – obviously as we are for the defence someone must go – we could send a solicitor.'

11

'Sir, something tells me Mr Dean should go in person.'

'It's Michael who's telling you that.' Honor was insistent. 'Michael himself.'

Sir George capitulated and picked up the telephone. 'Ginevra, please ask Mr Dean to come back.'

'Michael, the Lord God Almighty and Our Lady want you in His office.' Though Ginevra could be impertinent she was efficient and loyal – as were all the staff. As a matter of fact, 'lord' and 'lady' suited Sir George and Honor well: Sir George was imposing with his height and well-trimmed beard – 'Though not half as well tailored as Walter,' he used to say, because there were several expensive young Fothergills. Perhaps Walter, with his Savile Row suits and hand-made shoes, was trying to mitigate his own thickset stubbiness and grizzled hair. 'Well, even head clerks have their weaknesses,' said Sir George in sympathy. But no one could challenge Honor Wyatt, with her own height and imposing carriage, her fall of blonde hair – Michael remembered it drawn back into a knob, to hide it under the white barrister's wig, which seemed to make her features more clear. Her eyebrows were level, her grey eyes, too, although in court they could be as sharp as gimlets. She had an authority, a wit, that struck even Michael with awe: there could be no pretensions when he was with Honor. Now she, Sir George and Walter were waiting for him as he came in.

'You wanted me, Sir George?'

Sir George did not answer at once: he was looking at Michael as if he had never seen him before – Which he probably hasn't, thought Honor. 'Michael's made for this,' she had told Sir George, and added, as if she were thinking more deeply, 'He has hazel eyes.'

'What can that have to do with it?'

'Hazel eyes are mixed brown and grey, brown for earth and grey for—' she broke off. 'I'm only guessing but I think he can see further than we can.'

'With this case he'll need to,' said Sir George.

Michael, though he tried to restrain himself, was growing fidgety. 'You wanted me, Sir George,' he said again, and then as if he could not contain himself any longer, 'Oh, Sir George, I do so hope you've reconsidered.'

'I have reconsidered but not for myself. Michael, you'd better go and get your jabs. I gather you need a good many for India – typhoid, tetanus and I don't know what.'

'India?' Michael was almost speechless. 'You mean—'

'I mean go to your doctor at once.'

—◆—

The first thing Michael wanted to do was see the Nataraja, which still, for security reasons, in

Sparkes's, the famed art dealers', strongroom. 'Of course I will get you a pass,' Mr Bhatacharya had said. 'You can use it whenever you want, because I expect you will need to study the Nataraja closely.'

'As soon as I can,' Michael told him, 'but first I need a session with our head clerk.'

'The redoubtable Johnson? I wish I had someone like him in my office.'

'There's nobody like him,' said Michael.

—————

'I know you prefer finding things out for yourself,' Walter began, 'but you'll need a few facts. How much do you know about this Shiva?'

'I know it has at some time been taken out of India – been certified here as eleventh century. Finding it is surely a triumph after it has lain buried and undiscovered for all those years.'

'Not quite all,' said Walter. 'For some ninety years now, many people have known exactly where it was until it disappeared again. Mr Bhatacharya has told me the story as far as it goes and he had it from the woman, Mrs McIndoe – they call her Miss Sanni – who owns the hotel on the South Indian coast where the Shiva was housed.'

'An hotel?' Michael was surprised. 'How on earth – or should we say in heaven and earth? – did it get there?'

'If you'll listen,' said Walter severely, 'I'll tell you.'

14

'From where?'

'I'm coming to that, but I have to go back to the beginning as far as we know it. It may take time. I'll be as short as I can.'

'Not too short,' pleaded Michael. 'It's fascinating.'

'Very well, but I've warned you. In the early nineteen hundreds, say nineteen five or six, an Englishman, Henry Bertram, had made a fortune from indigo. All sailors' livery used to be dyed with it – all blue cloth. It grew like a weed in Bihar. But Bertram was an astute businessman. Chemical dyes were coming rapidly on the market and he sold his factory and fields just in time. He wanted to stay in India, so went to the east coast and built a luxury hotel – the only hotel in a most beautiful spot between the low hills and the beaches.

'He was even more astute than he knew, as it isn't far from the Sun Temple at Konak, the most beautiful in the world, in a region of temples. In the hills behind it there are rare ancient cave paintings and it made an ideal tourist centre, especially for the scholarly, while the beaches, too, are wonderful. As if he knew its future, he insisted on having what was rare in hotels at that time: a wine cellar and an ice-room in the basement, so that the workmen had to dig deep, so deep that they came upon the ruins of still another small temple.

'They refused to go on, begging Henry Bertram to choose another site. Like most English businessmen then, he knew nothing about Hinduism but he did know how to manage a workforce: he doubled their wages. But they had another reward. They found the little image of the Nataraja, lying face down, his hoop of flames unbroken. To propitiate them even more, when the hotel was finished Bertram had a niche built above the drawing-room-cum-ballroom door. I believe the Hindu servants and the villagers came to worship there and bring their offerings.'

'And he allowed them?'

'Always.'

'He must have been a remarkable man.'

'Yes, and he must, too, have had an affection for Bihar. He called his hotel Patna Hall – Patna is the capital of that state. The hotel is run now by Henry Bertram's granddaughter, Samantha.'

... 'Now?' she always said. 'I have been its manager since I was nine.' ...

'Henry Bertram brought her up,' Walter went on. 'There's no mention of parents. Though she married a Colonel McIndoe, Bhatacharya says everyone calls her Miss Sanni or, if you are close to her, Auntie Sanni. Colonel McIndoe, who does the business side, firmly installed electricity, telephones and a fax machine, but except for that Miss Sanni insists on keeping Patna Hall exactly as it was, in full old-time panoply, which must be very expensive. Indeed, Mr Bhatacharya thinks she finds it hard to keep it going, especially as he says India now has a chain of hotels,

the Uberois. "They are in every province," he told
me, "with high standards, comfortable and excellent
service, quick, which Patna Hall is decidedly not."
Yes, there's no fault to find with Uberois except that
all over India they're exactly the same – public rooms,
furnishings, even the menus. Most people stay at
them, but visitors say that if you've once been to
Patna Hall you want to come back again. An archae-
ological group has been coming every October for
the last twenty years. It's led now by a Professor Ellen
Webster who, I believe, is well known in America.
When she took it over the tour was only for women,
a mixture of holiday and sightseeing. Mr Bhatacharya
told me that the Patna Hall servants called them the
"cultural ladies", but now it's for men too and it's
considered a privilege to be accepted on one of these
tours – students get grants for them and people book
them from as far away as China.

'Professor Webster is meticulous,' Walter was
appreciative, 'and each year she comes to Patna Hall
a week or so in advance to check on every possible
arrangement. Mr Bhatacharya says this is very wise as
there is a proverb that Indians are so anxious to please
that they tell you things not as they are but as you
would like them to be – and now we come to the
point. On every tour there are evening lectures in
the ballroom. One is always on the Hindu deities
and, though no one else was allowed to touch it, Miss
Sanni let Professor Webster use the Nataraja, lifting it

17

down and putting it on her table. Last year the genuine statue was in place, but at some time during the last twelve months it has been exchanged.'

'And no one noticed?' Michael marvelled.

'The fake, they say, is exact,' said Walter, 'and remember, at Patna Hall everyone was used to seeing it in its niche. No, it took an Ellen Webster and she took the precaution of writing her discovery down.' He produced a page or two of manuscript and handed them to Michael.

As soon as I lifted it I knew it was a fake. The first thing was the weight. It was too light. Next the surface of the bronze was too smooth – no patina – and though it was so expertly made, something was missing, an ambience of calm, I can call it nothing else, a calm in spite of the dance. Of course I raised an alarm. I remember shouting, 'Auntie Sanni, Auntie Sanni! Come here at once. Call the Colonel. The Shiva's gone.'

'No. He is here.' Auntie Sanni had come, not hurrying.

'He's not. This is a fake. Someone's stolen yours. We must get the police at once.'

'There's no need for the police. He has not gone.'

'He has. He's gone! Gone! Gone!' I was trying to hammer it into Auntie Sanni. 'Gone.'

The confidential servants, Samuel the old

butler and Hannah the housekeeper, his wife, had come running. 'Aie! Aie! I get the police. I, Samuel.'

'No, Samuel,' said Miss Sanni. 'No, Ellen, let things be.'

'I can't. The Nataraja is not just yours. It's a national treasure, worth I don't know how much.'

Auntie Sanni was suddenly stern. 'I know what it's worth and I know the value, but not your kind of value or worth. Police, money, everything that disturbs. I forbid you, Ellen, absolutely forbid you to tell anyone. We still have our Shiva-ji.'

Michael read it closely. He looked up: 'What happened next?'

'Nothing for twenty-four hours, but the next day was the day when Mr Cromartie, a Canadian art dealer, arrived in London. He took the statue straight to Sparkes's. Soon there were mentions of it in some of the better English newspapers and the Indian ones immediately picked them up. Patna Hall's telephone rang incessantly. An enterprising journalist announced that he was coming. Miss Sanni had to give in: her prohibitions were no longer valid. "Do as you like," she said. Professor Webster had already written her formal testimony and lost no time in sending it to London.'

19

'Thank God for faxes,' Honor had said, when it arrived.

'It was certainly timely,' Walter told Michael. 'The Professor even offered to come to London as soon as her tour ended. The police made over the testimony at once to Mr Bhatacharya, who gave copies to everyone concerned. One is probably on its way to you. He told me he even gave one to Mr Cromartie, hoping he would drop this ridiculous case. But no. He's set on it.'

Michael came down to the snug again. 'Walter, have you a few minutes?'

'No,' said Walter, 'but I'll make some.'

'Thank you. Something has struck me about Cromartie versus the God Shiva, and I have a feeling that you know more than you let on about this man Cromartie.'

'Yes.' Then Walter was silent for a few moments. 'I was going to tell you when it seemed ripe but I don't think I behaved very well.'

'*You?*'

'Yes. Yet it was well before we were involved in the case. The Indian government and Mr Bhatacharya had not even approached Sir George, but when Mr Cromartie – Sydney Carstairs Cromartie, to give him his full name – had decided on litigation, he took action at once to find himself a lawyer. He seems not to have any friends or advisers in London, which doesn't surprise me, so he asked around. He said he wanted the best – and it appears that he's got plenty of money. Someone told him of us and he didn't wait a minute but came straight here demanding to see Sir George. Of course, he ended up with me.'

'What's he like?'

'Crass,' said Walter, without hesitation. 'Unbelievably ignorant because he's so cocksure he's always right. "I go my way and my way goes with me as it damn well has to" was one of his sayings. Ginevra didn't stand a chance – he was in the hall, had shut the door behind him and was flourishing his card at her before she could say a word. She still did her best. "Have you an appointment?"

'"Don't be silly, girl. I don't waste time making appointments. I have to see Sir Fothergill at once."'

Michael could not help laughing.

'It wasn't funny,' said Walter. 'Ginevra thought it better not to argue, but she's quick. She gave our invariable excuse, "Sir George is in court" and before Cromartie could speak she said, "If you'd like to leave your telephone number I'll get someone to call you as soon as possible." She got up to show him out but he stood between her and the door. She told me later she didn't like the look of him – well, he's certainly the reverse of attractive – and she really thought he might push straight past her so she showed him in to me. I expect he thought she'd capitulated and followed her quietly. "Someone to see you, Mr Johnson," she said, but one look at my snug and he was on the defensive. "You're not Sir Fothergill!"

'"Certainly not, Mr Cromartie." Ginevra had put his card, too flashy, on my desk. His name was in big letters but below, in smaller print, was "Ye Olde Oriental Treasure Chest" and an address in Toronto.'

'Ah!' Michael put in. 'Oriental Treasure Chest. That's the connection.'

'Obviously. The newspapers said the same. Anyway he attacked at once. "Sir George Fothergill's in court and, however urgent, he can't possibly be got out for me. That's the long and short of it, isn't it?" I had to agree, and he went on, "I'll tell you what I don't like – the way you English treat people from overseas as if they were bloody foreigners. I'm Canadian, mister, and Canada is part of the Commonwealth so we should be compatriots but I'm beginning to think that for us you're the bloody foreigners."

'Like Ginevra, I thought it better not to argue and there was a pause. Then Cromartie asked, "If I can't see Sir Fothergill who are you?" I told him my name and that I was head clerk to Sir George Fothergill's chambers,' and Walter added, 'I couldn't bring myself to call him sir.'

'"You don't look like a clerk," he said, so I told him again, head clerk. "I think you'll find, Mr Cromartie," I said, "that in chambers, even the heads work through their clerks, and so, Mr Cromartie, if you wish to see one of our barristers—" He interrupted me. "Sir George or no one. I won't have the girl."'

Walter, for once, had been moved to fury. 'The girl as you call her is Miss Honor Wyatt QC.'

'What in God's name's a QC?'

'Queen's Counsel, a very high rank of barrister. Anyway she couldn't take you. She's on an important case but, Mr Cromartie, to return to what I was going to tell you, if you want to see a barrister – certainly one of our barristers – your solicitor should make the appointment and accompany you.'

'Solicitor!' Cromartie exploded. 'So they told me but I'm not having any of that! I have no solicitor, Mr J., nor do I intend to have one. It's just another of your law-wallah's ruses to get money from a gullible public!'

As Michael heard that, he gasped. 'He said *that* in our chambers? Outrageous!'

'Yes, I nearly pressed the bell for Johnny and we would have propelled him out on to the street, but it wouldn't have been seemly – especially with all the notoriety of Miss Wyatt's Huntingdon case – so I let him go on.'

Cromartie had ranted, 'Well, I'm not gullible and you'll never make me have a solicitor.'

'Then you'll never see any of our barristers, nor, I can guess, any decent barrister,' had been Walter's response.

23

'That silenced him for a moment and I knew a struggle was going on in the man until he burst out, "Bloody blackmail!" Again I nearly pressed the bell for Johnny but Cromartie was evidently near the end of his tether and, sure enough, he almost wailed, "I must talk to *someone*. I wish I'd never seen that damned statue."

'It was pitiful. He was in such a state, his suit was crumpled – he was so paunchy it looked uncomfortably tight. His face was red with anger and he'd forgotten to brush his hair, which was ginger and clashed with the suit, which was a blatant bright brown – but there was no mistaking that he was genuine and I thought if I let him talk, asked him a few harmless questions, it might get rid of some of the spleen.'

'You're a kinder man than I am,' said Michael. 'I should have got Johnny at once, no matter what.'

'You'd have been right, but it seemed best at the time. I knew that the spleen was not only of rage but disappointment, not to say worry. Cromartie feels the whole world is against him and he doesn't know why, and he really *is* genuine. In fact, Michael, if this case does come on, I don't think you'll make mincemeat of him. He could get round a jury just as he nearly got round me.

'I began with what I thought was a safe question, "Do you have to travel a great deal for your Treasure Chest? To India perhaps?" but it made him even more belligerent.'

'I've never been to India in my life, and I don't want to!' Cromartie had bellowed. 'I bought the statue right there in Toronto where I do my business – successfully I'm glad to say. Mister, I run this small shop – exclusive, mind you – for which I buy Oriental goods. I have my sources. What's wrong with that?'

'Nothing, as long as you know where the goods come from, but do you always?'

'How could I? In my trade you don't ask questions. Anyway if you did you wouldn't be told the truth. A chap came to see me, bringing the statue. You people treat me as if I were an idiot but I tell you, the moment I saw it I knew it was different, though I didn't know how different. He said he'd bought it in India from a workman who'd found it buried.'

To Michael, Walter added, 'Well, as you know, that happened to be true.'

Mr Cromartie had gone on, 'The fellow called himself Narayan Gupta. Of course, he haggled over the price, but I couldn't get him below twenty-five thousand dollars – more than I ever paid for anything in my life. Of course I never saw the fellow again.'

'We could trace him through the cheque.'

Mr Cromartie had given Walter a pitying look. 'I paid him cash.'

'Cash? Twenty-five thousand? Didn't that make you suspicious?'

'It's the custom. How Mr Narayan Gupta keeps his accounts is nothing to do with me.'

'It was convincing,' Walter told Michael, 'but somehow I felt I must persist so I asked him, "You are sure, Mr Cromartie, that the Shiva is yours to sell?" and for the first time, there was a moment's hesitation until he said reluctantly, "Granted there was some hanky-panky."

'"Dishonesty," I told him flatly.

'"Not on my part. Didn't I get a licence to bring the statue over? Declared it to customs. It cost me a bomb, I can tell you, but I had to get it valued."'

Michael interrupted, 'Toronto has the Royal Ontario Museum with a wonderful oriental department. Why didn't he go there?'

'He did, but only to ask them if they'd tell him who were the best dealers for oriental antiques. To give him his due, Mr Cromartie doesn't do things by halves. Of course they said Sparkes's. He booked the next flight to London.'

Michael had been brooding as he listened. 'Cromartie said, "Damned statue." I don't like to think of him with the Shiva.'

'Neither do I, but it wasn't for long. As soon as he was free of Customs, even before he'd found an hotel, he put the Shiva into a taxi and took it to Sparkes's and, in Cromartie fashion, demanded a table or a stand, took the statue out of its case, set it there and told the dumbfounded salesman to fetch the manager who, surprisingly, came – I expect the salesman had said something to him. Soon two or three others were summoned, and a young woman. Cromartie saw they were deeply impressed.'

'Of course I was gratified,' he had admitted to Walter, 'I told them how and where I got the statue, but not, of course, what I paid. Then I asked them straight out, "How much do you think you could get me for it?" In this country it seems no one can answer a question directly. They hummed and hawed. "It will take time, Mr Cromartie" . . . "We'll have to be sure" . . . "Get expert advice". . . "Maybe consult the Indian government" . . . and finally, "If you leave it with us . . ."'

'"No way," I told them.'

'"It would be safer than in an hotel – we have a strongroom," they said. "Of course you would have a receipt." Oh, they went on until I said, "I'll leave it with you for two days, no more." And what did they do?' Mr Cromartie had burst out in fury again. 'They called in the police, without a word of reference to me.'

'That was a bit hard,' said Michael.

'I thought so too,' said Walter, 'but I said, trying to smooth things over, "Perhaps they thought if they'd told you, you'd have taken it away."'

'God's truth I would!' Mr Cromartie had been emphatic. 'It's mine, isn't it? Yet they treated me as if I was a receiver of stolen goods.'

'Perhaps you were – unwittingly.'

'There you go. You too!' Mr Cromartie said bitterly.

'I said *unwittingly*,' Walter reminded him.

'And so you should. Haven't I told you and told you? From the day I first saw the statue I have behaved with complete openness throughout. *Throughout*,' Mr Cromartie had emphasized again. 'That's more than can be said for Mr Bhata– I can never remember their names. The man they sent for from India.'

'Mr Bhatacharya. We know of him. He's a senior official.'

'He may be. I thought at first he was trustworthy, but he's glib as hell. He was sent here immediately the British police informed the Government of India. He told me he'd been authorized to reimburse me for the money I'd paid and the same again, and all in pounds not dollars, as a thank-you for bringing the statue so openly to London. A "thank you", I don't think.'

'But you accepted it,' Walter had demurred.

'Then, not now. Then it seemed quite good to me. Fifty thousand pounds is not to be sneezed at – pounds not dollars. But I'd put nothing in writing. We Cromarties are not fools, mister, and, sure enough, I found the Government of India had tried cheating me. The experts, especially that Sir Lennox from the British Museum, valued the little piece at at

least a quarter of a million pounds. Two hundred and
fifty thousand, mark you. And said he'd be glad to
pay even more to have the statue in his museum.'

'Of course he can't. It's got to go back to India,'
Walter said.

'So it will, if they pay me for it – the proper price
which, mind you, they knew all along, not a paltry
fifty thousand. They're trying to cheat me. You can't
deny it, though I think you're trying to persuade me
that I have no case. Of course I have. Haven't I
checked and rechecked?'

'Beyond all doubt?' Walter had asked, and said
now to Michael, 'I felt I had to drive that in and I
said, "Mr Cromartie, you're not on certain ground.
If at any point the Shiva had been stolen it wouldn't
be yours to sell. You've read Professor Ellen Webster's testimony, which is beyond all doubt, so maybe
fifty thousand was generous."'

'Was it?' Mr Cromartie had snapped. 'What if I
told you I know something that you, smart Mr J., her
and even Mr Bhata don't know.' He had come so close
that Walter could smell his breath – 'And himself,
ugh,' he told Michael. 'It was very disagreeable.'

'A young man came to see me.' Mr Cromartie
had been almost whispering. 'He had read in the
papers about my bringing the statue to London. His
name is Kanu and he's much closer to Mrs McIndoe
– Miss Sanni of that hotel – than any visiting
professor. He was practically brought up at Patna

Hall. He says Miss Sanni was like a mother to him. Kanu is now nineteen and has been working at Patna Hall as barman and receptionist – staff there have to double up, these days. His great ambition, though, is to be a barman at one of the Uberoi hotels, and to help him Mrs McIndoe sent him to London for a short intensive training course.

... "For an Uberoi you need it," Kanu had said. "All Uberois first class, modern, not like running-down old hotel ..."

'It seems,' Mr Cromartie went on, 'that Patna Hall is in financial trouble and he swears that the stealing of the Shiva statue was only a pretence. In fact, it was carefully planned, and by whom? This Mrs McIndoe – good old Miss Sanni herself. She had the fake one made – Kanu says she knows every image-maker or sculptor in the region. It was she who switched the statues and – I guess under her colonel husband's advice – sent it to be sold. Kanu says he understands: "She did it to save Patna Hall."'

'Hm,' Walter had said. 'Who told him that?'

'I assume Mrs McIndoe.' Mr Cromartie was haughty now.

'In a court case,' Walter said, 'we can't assume. We have to prove.'

'Isn't it proof?' Mr Cromartie had argued. 'Kanu was privy to everything. She treated him like a son.'

'So he says, but mothers don't tell their sons everything, nor sons their mothers.'

'But don't you see? You all seem to set such store by this Professor's testimony but Kanu's story explains why Mrs McIndoe wouldn't let anyone call the police and wanted it all to be kept hush-hush. It fits like a glove. You can't deny that.'

'I don't, but from what I've heard of her it doesn't fit Miss Sanni.'

'Why?'

'Kanu himself says the hotel is in financial difficulty yet she finds the money to send him on an expensive course – they always are expensive – just to help him further his ambitions. That sounds beneficent to me and not like someone who would make the statue vanish and blame it on someone else. As for Kanu, if she did tell him in confidence, he took the first opportunity to betray her. Mr Cromartie, why do you think he told you?'

'For money,' Mr Cromartie had said, as if that explained everything.

'Then,' said Walter, 'for money he would betray you too. No, Mr Cromartie, I'm sure Sir George Fothergill would advise you not to proceed with this case.'

'Drop it? When I've just discovered—'

'It's too tricky. You might lose a lot of money.'

'That's my business, so don't bloody well try to talk me out of it. I have a watertight case. The statue was *not* stolen and I am *not* a receiver of stolen goods.'

'I had one more try,' Walter told Michael. 'I felt I had to.'

. . . 'Mr Cromartie, I admire your courage but you will have the whole weight of the Government of India against you, and they've brought in an added power, the God Shiva.'

'I don't listen to that sort of crap.'

'No, but a jury might if it comes to it. In law, we're taught to respect other people's beliefs, and the God Shiva has great influence.'

'Balls!' . . .

'And he left as suddenly as he'd come,' Walter finished.

'I think he ran away,' said Michael, and cried, 'Hail, Shiva, *Jai Shiv Shankara*.'

Now, to see the Nataraja Michael had to be provided with an official pass. 'They have to know exactly who you are,' Mr Bhatacharya had told him. The police had left the Shiva in Sparkes's strongroom, 'Where it couldn't be more safe, and we have given them a security guard round the clock.'

Michael's arms ached from the inoculations and one had swollen, but with every prick he had felt more alert, expectant.

He made his way to a high old building in the quiet of St James's Place. Premises seemed the right word for Sparkes's. Michael knew it was one of the world's chief specialists in oriental sculpture, paint-ings, *objets d'art*: Cromartie chose well, he thought. A commissionaire in a braided uniform was standing outside.

Michael was early, and spent the time looking in the windows. Though they were high and of plate glass, they were almost empty. In one was a sixth-century bronze incense burner. But for the card Michael would not have known what it was. The next window held only a Chinese ivory fan lying spread in all its delicacy on a length of crimson brocade, but another had a vast Tibetan banner with flowers, demons and flames in brilliant colours. Michael stood, trying to take it in, until the commissionaire beckoned him.

Inside it was more like a salon than a shop. He was met by a polished and poised young woman. 'Mr Dean? Good morning. I'm Julia Macdonald and I look after our smaller artifacts.' She offered him tea: 'China or herbal?' Out of curiosity Michael chose herbal. It came in small, handleless jade cups and he could not help thinking, Miss Julia, you're showing off.

'You're the barrister for the defence?' she was saying. 'Have you met Mr Cromartie?'

'No, but I gather he's not the kind of client Sparkes's would enjoy.'

'Well, I felt we were a bit high-handed. I'm surprised he isn't suing us. There was quite a scene.' Julia Macdonald laughed then sobered. 'And he did bring us the Nataraja, but here I am wasting your time when you must be longing to see it.'

Michael got up with alacrity – the herbal tea had been disgusting.

She called to the commissionaire and he brought in another man, who led the way down a flight of steps to a narrow passage without windows – Michael guessed it was below the shop. Then, in a small hall or vault, they were faced with double steel doors which the man opened with a combination of keys. The room behind was instantly lit, flooded with light by inset rays from overhead and along the walls. In the centre, set on a high table that fitted its plinth, was the Shiva, dancing in his hoop of miniature flames. Michael caught his breath.

The Nataraja seemed far larger than it was, dominating the room. The dancing limbs were naked in eternal energy. 'The drum in his upper right hand makes the primordial sound of creation,' whispered Julia Macdonald. 'His left upper arm holds a flame, the flame of destruction, while the left points to his dancing left foot, which means release, and he is treading on a dwarf who lies prostrate, the dwarf of all ignorance and prejudice. Shiva wears men's and women's jewellery because although he had wives, his attachment to the world is without gender.'

Michael nearly said, 'Hush.' He wanted only to look. '"Statue" is too still a word for this. He's living,' he whispered, as if to himself but it stopped Julia.

'Shiva *is* life,' she whispered back.

'Yes, look at his face, utterly detached, yet there's something in-dwelling.' Michael stopped in surprise. 'That's an odd word for me to use.'

'It's exactly right.' There was no trace of the polished, poised, a little pretentious Miss Macdonald. 'I come in here every night before I go home to find out what it is, but of course – it *is* in-dwelling. Yes, I might even bring him marigold garlands.' She had recovered herself, and as Michael left, she said, 'Mr Cromartie swears he bought the Nataraja in good faith. Maybe he did. Anything may happen but I know I wish . . .'

'Wish what?'

'That Shiva should go back to where he belongs. India.'

'I can only try,' said Michael.

'So you leave tomorrow?'

'Yes,' said Michael. 'I still can't believe it.' He had come to say goodbye to Sir George and Honor.

'Have you all you need? Walter given you your papers?'

'Everything, sir. I think he'd quite like to come.'

'I can't imagine that!' Honor laughed.

Sir George got up – he did not believe in protracting things. 'Well, goodbye and good luck. I'm sure you'll do well.'

'If I can have a free hand.' Michael was Michael to the last.

'Good God!' Sir George expostulated, when Michael had gone. 'There's conceit for you – laying down conditions!'

'George, he has to. He has no idea what he'll find. Nor have we, but to do your best you have to believe in your case. I'm sure Michael does and will fight for it, no matter what it costs him. Isn't Michael the fighting angel?'

INDIA

IN HIS HIRED car, an Indian-made Ambassador, Michael drove from the airport at Ghandara, Patna Hall's nearest small town, along a dusty golden plain where white oxen were ploughing small fields and the road was filled with people, rickshaws and little black-and-gold three-wheeled taxis he did not remember having seen before. Then he came through a pair of great open gates, under a tall portico.

The first thing he heard as he got out of the car was the sound of the sea, although the portico faced inland. There seemed no one about so, taking his briefcase which he always kept with him, he walked round the house to find the beach.

The hotel stood high on its plinth of basements, which Michael knew held Henry Bertram's wine cellar and ice room. The house itself was painted blue, now faded, a tribute to the indigo, and a wide flight of steps led to the lower veranda – as he looked up there seemed to be two, one on each floor stretching its full length. The flat roof was parapeted but he could see more rooms up there.

As he walked round, he discovered that Patna

Hall was quite a demesne. There were domestic quarters, and, though he did not know it then, a separate house for the two head servants, Samuel and Hannah. There was a gatehouse, a side court with a row of offices, a large vegetable garden, a poultry yard, even a private cemetery. Behind the hotel was the village, but all Michael could see of it were palms and a few thatched roofs.

On the other side of the house, facing the sea, was a garden with a wide lawn, beds of English and Indian flowers and a path of stepping stones bordered with shells that led down to the hotel's private, netted beach. As he walked down towards it the sound of the surf was a roar. He followed the stones and came on to dry white sands that stretched away on either side into dunes of feathery trees. Tamarisk, he guessed, and behind them were what he thought must be mango groves.

Beyond the sea had lost its sunlight and was beginning to glimmer. On the foreshore of hard wet sand, the great rollers of the Coromandel coast rose – he was amazed at their height – and crashed down, sending ripples far up the sand almost to his feet.

'Sahib, I think you get your feet wet.'

It was a man's voice, deep toned and speaking English; a giant of a man. It was too dark to see clearly but even in the fading light his skin was brown gold. He wore nothing but a loincloth and a short white *chaddar* shoulder wrap, and hanging from his hands were local fishermen's helmets, made of woven wicker, immensely strong with a pointed peak, to break the waves – otherwise they stun you, Michael learned. The man was hanging them on a rail to dry. 'For hotel bathing guests,' he explained. 'I Thambi, Patna Hall lifeguard.'

He spoke English slowly, as if he had by heart what he needed to say. 'If Sahib swim tomorrow I help him.' He gestured towards a high diving tower and a stack of surf boards.

'Thank you, I will,' said Michael.

There was a pause until Thambi said, 'I am thinking you must be legal gentleman from England.' He laughed. 'And I thinking, too, that he will be important, older, with spectacles and perhaps a beard.'

'I'm sorry.'

'No, I like, and pleased to see you. Miss Sanni very not happy about it at all.'

'So you know about the case?'

'Everybody know it. How not?'

'But you have no idea who did it?'

At once Michael sensed a caginess. For all his impressive presence, a lifeguard was a servant at Patna Hall. It isn't a cliché, thought Michael, to say that no one knows more about their masters than those who serve them, but he was sure that if Thambi knew anything about the Shiva he was not going to tell.

The sun was now completely gone. A little chill

wind blew. Thambi gave a shiver. 'I think better I take you to hotel.' They walked up the stone path, then he showed Michael round to the portico and opened the car boot, took out the suitcase and brought it into the hall. 'I put car away. Reception is there. Salaam, Sahib.'

—◦—

The hall was panelled, as was the staircase leading up from it. Doors opened into the ground-floor veranda and the dining room. There was a fine grandfather clock, two carved low chests, and behind a long counter a young Indian waited with his telephone and ledgers. He was formally dressed, wearing a collar and tie – there was nothing casual about the service at Patna Hall. Kanu, Michael guessed.

'Good evening, Mr Dean. We are expecting you. If you would just sign here, and I must have your passport, please. May I say welcome. Please call me Kanu.'

To Michael, there was something too glib – as if Kanu was copying what he had learned on his course in London. He was very good-looking, in a childish way – the thick hair that must have been curly once, long eyelashes, the charming smile, which vanished as a door opened. 'Auntie Sanni is coming. She always like to welcome guests herself.' He sounded a little peevish.

Kanu should not have said 'Auntie Sanni'. To her

staff and most guests she was Miss Sanni. 'Auntie', in Eurasian parlance, is the title given by children to any grown-up female, but with Mrs McIndoe not everyone was allowed to use it, and before she spoke to Michael, she said sharply, 'Kanu, you should be at the bar. Go and put on your jacket at once.' Then she advanced. 'Mr Dean, we are so very glad to meet you.'

Michael saw a massive old woman wearing what he was to recognize as one of her usual voluminous cotton dresses that hung like a tent to her feet; she called them her Mother Hubbards, from the garments missionaries used to hand out to make the native women what they called respectable. 'Well, I am a native,' she would tell Michael. She had country sandals: 'They suit me and are very comfortable.' She said 'very' in the Eurasian way so that it became 'veree' with a little lift. 'Well, I expect I am Eurasian. I expect my mother was Indian, maybe her mother. I never knew them. He didn't marry my mother.'

'Did you want him to?'

'Why? That's men's business.'

To Sir George she would have been illegitimate, but to Auntie Sanni it was 'natural'. Her skin was of the mixed-race complexion, the pale yellowish brown of old ivory and unwrinkled which, though she was old, made her look young. Eternally young, thought Michael, with her head of short curls, still auburn and glossy, while her eyes looked curiously

43

light, sea-colour, now green, now blue. Mixed, like mine, thought Michael, but set wide like a child's, although again he was to learn, as every perspicacious person who came to Patna Hall and every business person with whom she dealt soon learnt, while, above all, every servant and villager knew, that Auntie Sanni was no child.

'And so you have come about this unfortunate case.' Michael knew that the sea-blue eyes were taking him in – not only from head to foot, but heart and soul. He had not thought, until this case, that he believed in souls.

'I hope I can help,' he said, 'but I've come really to help me understand.'

'There could be no greater help,' said Auntie Sanni, 'no greater,' she said. It was mysterious that at once he had ceased to think of her as Miss Sanni, certainly not as Mrs McIndoe. 'Mr Dean, I have to confess that this case is very objectionable to me, but come, we will not talk of it tonight. You must be tired. Hannah, our housekeeper, will show you to your room. We have put you in a bedroom on the front where you can catch the sea breezes. Then perhaps you will join me and my husband, Colonel McIndoe, at our veranda bar and have a drink before dinner. Ah! Here is Hannah come to show you upstairs. She and her husband, Samuel, are the pillars of Patna Hall.'

Hannah was a big woman, though not compared

with her mistress. She wore a crisp white cotton sari, bordered with red, and an old-fashioned red bodice high on the neck. Her scant grey hair was pinned in a knob at the back of her head, but in spite of this simplicity she was laden with silver jewellery: the lobes of her ears hung down with the weight of earrings, she had several necklaces, bracelets, finger rings, and toe rings on her gnarled bare feet. She beckoned to a houseboy in white trousers and brass-buttoned tunic, with a small round black embroidered hat on his head, who ran down the stairs to carry Michael's suitcase. Once again Michael did not let his briefcase out of his hand.

They showed him to a high-ceilinged room off the top veranda, with a mosquito-netted bed, wardrobe, dressing-table and stool, a comfortable wicker chair, a table, flowers, a newspaper. Everything, thought Michael. 'Give Kancha your keys,' suggested Hannah as Michael stepped outside to look at the view. Before he came back, filled with it, Kancha had unpacked, putting things orderly in drawers, hair brushes on the dressing table, ties on a rack, jackets and trousers on hangers; he was already laying out on the bed a clean shirt and the fine linen suit Michael had instinctively brought. 'As I had guessed,' he wrote later to Honor, 'at Patna Hall we dress for dinner.'

When he had bathed and changed he did not go straight down but stopped again on the high veranda outside his room and looked far over the garden to the dark sea, quiet now, only the rollers glimmering white in the starlight. He stood there a moment, feeling cleansed and fresh, letting the breeze blow cool through his hair. It brought a scent of flowers, strong and sweet, and the hours of travel, closed in the small plastic world of aeroplanes, dropped away. Then, A drink would be nice, and he turned to the stairs, but at their foot he paused. Why not explore?

The rooms were all high and floored with red stone. Michael looked into the dining room, where it was evident that a ritual was going on: tables being meticulously laid by white-clad waiters, vases, each holding a single rose, brought in. The stone shone: indeed, every morning a posse of village women came in to sit on the floor, moving slowly backwards as they pushed empty wine bottles, their bases wrapped in waxed cloth, until it gleamed.

'One electric polisher could do the work of twelve women,' said Kanu.

'I know, but I like to employ as many villagers as I can.' Auntie Sanni was quite comfortable.

Now, a humble woman, her sari drawn over her head, was giving the floor a last sweep because, to Samuel's grief, if the wind were high, sand blew in over it. Of the great Samuel himself there was no sign: he, too, was changing into a fresh white uniform for dinner.

There was a billiard room with a good table,

empty now; it had a bar in one corner. Perhaps, thought Michael, gentlemen, chiefly Indians, would come in from Ghandara to play, have a few drinks or perhaps bring their ladies for dinner, but the veranda bar, he imagined, was reserved for residents.

The drawing room–ballroom was away from the rest, an immense double room. Its floor was green as, though paler, were the walls, lit by crystal-beaded candle sconces – Henry Bertram certainly didn't stint himself, thought Michael. A matching chandelier hanging in the centre of the room bore this out. Auntie Sanni had chosen a rather naïve sweet-pea chintz for the sofas and chairs, and there were small brass-topped tables on carved ebony legs. Over the ornate marble fireplace was a not very good painting of a young girl – plump even then – in a 1920s ball dress, pale blue with sequins. The auburn curls were held in a circlet of small pink roses and she had a bouquet to match. A coming-out ball? wondered Michael. It was plain that Henry Bertram had been proud of his granddaughter.

It was a room that was evidently used for occasions. Did Patna Hall host weddings? Receptions? But he guessed, Seldom now, and when he dared to turn on the electric fans they creaked, yet he could see it filled with people in elegant dress, dancing or chattering and laughing. Then, as he turned to go, he saw the Shiva Nataraja.

In a niche above a side door that opened onto the

veranda steps to the sea, the Nataraja danced, a votive light burning before him with offerings of flowers, fruit and rice. As Michael looked he was transported back to Sparkes's strongroom and saw again the beauty and strength of what he had come to call 'the real Nataraja'. At first he saw no difference between that and this but exact as this Shiva was, to the last little flare in the circlet of flames around His head, and although there was still a feeling of steadiness, well captured, there was no aura of that inward strength of detachment, that in-dwelling. Well, this Shiva had been made by a craftsman, but no more than a craftsman, and Michael's thoughts went to that true artist-sculptor of centuries ago.

'You are looking at the Shiva.' The voice made him jump. Auntie Sanni was standing beside him.

She, too, had changed, into a clean Mother Hubbard, white scattered with bright blue flowers – Auntie Sanni loved colours. She wore her pearl necklace, the pearls real and beautifully matched; the curls had been brushed hard and her toenails polished. Hannah, he was to find, was not only housekeeper but Auntie Sanni's personal maid. Every evening when she was dressed, Colonel McIndoe in his heavy silk dinner jacket – in the hot weather a silk cummerbund – came to fetch her and escort her to her swinging couch on the bar veranda, 'Her throne,' mocked Kanu. Michael guessed this was, like so much at Patna Hall, the evening ritual, yet now she

48

was alone. 'I still say, "Our Shiva-ji",' she told Michael. 'I'm the only one who does.'

'You still say it?'

'Every morning. Every night. He is still Shiva.'

'Auntie Sanni.' Then Michael remembered he was still a newcomer. 'May I call you Auntie Sanni?'

'If I may call you Michael.'

'Of course. Will you tell me what happened?'

'You have read Professor Ellen's testimony?' she asked.

'Yes, but underneath . . .'

'Ah! Underneath. There are things she doesn't know. My grandfather, Henry Bertram, was a wonderful man. When Shiva-ji was found buried and the workmen refused to go on my grandfather did not double their wages as has been told but sent for their priest to unearth the little statue and turn it round. The men did not dare to touch it but most Englishmen then would have stepped in and got it. After prayers the priest turned it gently and then lifted it up. Usually statues which have been long buried – and this had been so for centuries – are crusted with soil and stone, particularly by the sea, and there could have been termites, but the Nataraja came up as clean as on the day he was buried, the limbs still dancing, each flame intact. Above all, His face was serene and smiling.

'The workmen prostrated themselves and my

grandfather promised that this little shrine would be made in our most important room to which not only the house servants but all the villagers could come and worship. The workmen refused to take another *anna* for their work to build the hotel which, of course, meant,' she added laughing, 'he had to keep their families for months.'

'He must have been a remarkable man,' said Michael, for the second time.

'He was, and what would he have said now to this horrible Cromartie case?'

'It must be horrible to you too. Walter Johnson, the head clerk at our chambers, saw Mr Cromartie and tried to persuade him not to bring it.'

'He deserves to lose. He must lose. I have no pity for Mr Cromartie,' said Auntie Sanni. 'He says he bought the Shiva Nataraja in good faith. That is not true. Good faith would mean he bought it to love and revere. Oh, no! He bought it to make money, *invested* in it, and now, because he has not made the profit he expected, he is prosecuting, and so denigrating the god even more. Also he is a fool. My grandfather always said, "Beware of litigation."'

'So beware of me,' said Michael.

Auntie Sanni looked up into his face, then took his hands with both her own. 'I think I need not beware of you, Michael. I know now we are in this together. Now, come. You must meet my husband

and the few others who are staying here – old friends except the policeman.'

'The policeman?'

'Yes. I'll tell you later.'

But Michael stopped for a moment. 'Auntie Sanni, don't you mind about the fake?'

'It is not a fake. It was time for our Shiva-ji Nataraja to move on. He had other work to do, but very kindly he left himself behind, for us. Come,' said Auntie Sanni.

—◆—

The veranda bar was the residents' sitting place, with cane chairs and tables, cane stools, old-fashioned steamer chairs with extended arm boards on which feet could be comfortably put up. There was a bar at one end, well stocked. 'Well, we get visitors from all parts of the world,' Auntie Sanni would say, and half-way down was her swing couch, with its bright chintz cushions and canopy. It was true that before lunch, which she called 'tiffin', and before dinner she liked to sit there and reign. Now a small group of people were sitting round one of the cane tables near Auntie Sanni's throne. All old, thought Michael, with a touch of dismay. One of the oldest, the lights shining on his bald head, got up at once, came to Michael and shook hands.

'I am Samantha's husband,' he said, no one else used that name, 'Colonel McIndoe. We're glad to see you here. Kanu,' he called, 'get the sahib a drink. Whisky, gin, vodka, a glass of wine?'

Kanu, transformed by a striped cotton jacket, came at once.

'Whisky, please. Thank you, sir.'

Kanu looked at him surprised. Perhaps because I called the Colonel 'sir', thought Michael, as Auntie Sanni began, 'Alicia, this is Mr Dean come to help us over this miserable affair. He wants us to call him Michael. Michael, Lady Fisher is one of our oldest friends.'

'You must be tired,' Lady Fisher said gently, but then, 'No. You young people are never tired.'

'Not when we're on the scent, I suppose,' said Michael. 'I'm so glad it has brought me here.'

'Patna Hall has brought us every year, hasn't it, Sanni?' There was clearly a deep friendship here. 'My husband and I. John, this is Michael Dean,' and Michael knew there was some familiarity about Sir John, his height, the silvery – cliché or not he could not help thinking it – 'silvery' hair. He's like someone I know. Sir John immediately confirmed it. 'You're from the chambers of Sir George Fothergill? I'm glad. Good set. I have a niece there.'

'Honor Wyatt.' Michael was certain.

'Yes, in fact I was able to be instrumental in bringing her to your chambers. I used to know Simpson well and, of course, that wonderful head clerk, John Johnson.'

'We have his son Walter now, and Johnny, Walter's son, has just joined us. Walter's a great advocate for Honor.'

'I don't wonder. She's an outstanding young woman.'

'John,' Lady Fisher interposed, 'Mr Dean hasn't been introduced to Ellen or Chief Inspector Dutta. Professor Ellen Webster,' and 'Ellen, I think you've been expecting Mr Dean?'

'Indeed I have.'

She was a small, over-thin woman – Probably works too hard, thought Michael, and is too intense. Michael could never help analysing everything. The Professor was pale, her hair cut into neat shortness, grey eyes behind steel-rimmed spectacles, an almost anonymous blouse and skirt. She doesn't care about superficial things, thought Michael.

'You're going to help us save our Nataraja.' She held his hand, looking up at him closely, and he knew that here was a heartfelt passion, though she had learned how to keep it cool. 'Mr Dean, this is Chief Inspector Dutta of the Indian police.'

'I didn't know that they had been called in,' said Michael, as he shook hands.

'I am always called in.' The Inspector chuckled. Younger than any of these guests, he was still middle-aged and plump and genial, but Michael sensed at once that Inspector Dutta was not a chief inspector for nothing. Though dressed for the evening, he still seemed to be in uniform, thin trousers and a tunic jacket, both khaki, and a red scarf round his neck in lieu of a tie. 'I am necessarily here,' he explained. 'Our government has decided that we must outface Mr Cromartie and must have positive proof that the image was stolen. Forgive me, Professor Webster, if I say that your testimony, though so valuable, is still not positive proof, besides which it was written so long after the theft. We must discover when, how and, above all, by whom the Bertram Nataraja as it has begun to be named, was taken.'

'I should think very difficult after all these months,' said Sir John.

The Inspector laughed. 'Set a thief to catch a thief. I am an accomplished one, stealing shreds of evidence wherever I can and weaving them together until I understand fully.' There was a hint of menace in the way he said that; then he was jovial again. 'I'll catch him.'

'Michael,' Auntie Sanni obviously wanted to end that conversation, 'you must be thinking our hotel is over-quiet and empty but tomorrow it will be much better as Professor Webster's group will be arriving.'

And to Michael's surprise the Colonel, Sir John and Lady Fisher chanted, 'The cultural ladies, the cultural ladies.'

'Don't be alarmed, Michael,' said Auntie Sanni. 'Before Professor Ellen's day that's what Samuel and Hannah used to call them, not mockingly – they have a great reverence for learning.'

'Since Ellen took over it has completely changed, with many men now, and it's considered a privilege to be accepted for a tour – students get grants. I believe we shall have a Chinese girl on this one,' said Lady Fisher.

For the first time Michael looked, really looked, at Lady Fisher. When she spoke it was with authority but most of the time she sat quietly, her eyes alight with interest as she listened to what everyone was saying. He guessed that was her greatest asset, listening, and a rare talent. Sir John had a sun-tanned, wrinkled skin from years in the tropics, but Lady Fisher, who had spent all of them with him, had a complexion that looked as if strong sun or a rough wind had never touched it. 'Alicia prefers not to go on the beach or bathe, or lie in the sun,' Auntie Sanni said to Michael, who was sitting on the swing couch beside her.

'Then why does she come to a seaside hotel?'

'To be with John. Has it never occurred to you, Michael, that some eminent men, with pressures of work, tangles of worries, disappointments and horrendous surprises, need a calm, steadfast and highly intelligent wife? Sir John thinks he is taking care of her but she is really taking care of him.'

'Well, Ellen,' Sir John persisted, 'when they come, I'll leave.'

'Nonsense, John.'

Lady Fisher said, 'I grant you that, in the old days,

the ladies were a bit of a bore but Ellen's here now and Artemis has flown out from London to bring them from New York. The tours always begin and end in New York. Artemis is Ellen's assistant.'

'Assistant! She's my star. No wonder, John, you always fall for her,' Professor Ellen teased him.

'Artemis is a witch,' admitted Sir John.

'I've never known a girl called that,' said Michael. 'Isn't it a bit fanciful?'

'I think it's a lovely name,' said Lady Fisher.

'And she's a lovely girl,' said Professor Ellen.

'So, John, you're not to forget how things have moved on and call the women old tabbies.' Lady Fisher turned to Inspector Dutta. 'They're such inspiring tours. I wish more young people could get grants for them. I think your government ought to support them. Can't you use your influence?'

'I have no influence. I do only what I am told.'

'That I don't believe,' and Professor Ellen went on, 'In fact, since you came to Patna Hall I am sure, over the Nataraja, you're on the same side as Michael and all of us.'

'This detestable case!' Auntie Sanni burst out. 'It was you, Ellen, who told me – and everyone else – what our Shiva-ji was worth in value of money and that seems to me the beginning of the trouble. Since then everything has gone wrong.'

'It seems so,' Professor Ellen said miserably.

Auntie Sanni was shaking, tears running down her

face. Lady Fisher got up, went to her and put an arm round her, holding her close. At the same moment Samuel sounded the gong.

'I'll tell him to hold dinner back a few minutes.' Colonel McIndoe was up, but nothing could have revived Auntie Sanni more.

'No. No, Giles. You can't do that to Samuel. Nor can I.' She stood up too. Lady Fisher had given her a handkerchief and she dabbed her eyes. 'Dinner is ready,' and she and the Colonel led the way to the dining room.

That was always a proud moment for Samuel. He stood at the entrance, regal in his flowing white tunic, full trousers, and red and gold cummerbund. His white turban, with its fan of white muslin, was held by a narrower crossband, red and gold to match, with a glittering Bertram crest. His whiskers and upturned moustache were white too, his eyes alert to every least movement.

It was understood that they went to different tables. Professor Ellen was with Auntie Sanni and the Colonel, the Fishers had their own corner and Inspector Dutta turned to Michael. 'We are both alone. Shall we eat together, Mr Dean?'

'I'd like that, but please call me Michael.'

'Then I am Hem.'

Samuel had anticipated this, and led them across the room to a table already laid for two.

'Now you must want to pump me,' the Inspector

said, as they took their seats, 'but you will be wasting your time. The food here is too good to think of anything else.'

The table itself was inviting: the single rose was a fine one and, in china soup plates with the Bertram crest, a chilled raisin soup waited, rich brown and refreshing.

'I am, I admit, impressed,' Inspector Dutta said, 'particularly because I have seen how it is all achieved. Miss Sanni does not believe in change. In Patna Hall's pantry there are packing cases lined with zinc, a small brazier burning red to keep food hot and an army of boys to run with dishes between the kitchen, which is outside, and the house.'

Hot plates were slipped in front of them and Samuel himself waited on them. 'Koftas,' he explained to Michael, 'little batter rolls of fish. Crayfish. Very good.'

Michael discovered he was starving while Hem Dutta said, 'I should very much like to give you some wine but, Michael, you choose. Europeans know much more of wine than us ignorant Indians.'

'Ignorant! Hem, don't put me to shame. It's we who are ignorant of your great country.'

'Choose,' said the Inspector, and when the wine list came, Michael was careful to find something good but among the less expensive – he had no idea how much an Indian policeman, even a chief inspector, earned. Then his dilemma was solved: Samuel brought a bottle of cool white wine, already opened – 'From Miss Sanni.' He poured it.

Michael stood up to thank her. 'To Miss Sanni and Patna Hall.' Everyone drank.

The hotel served a menu of both Indian and European food. The koftas were followed by partridges on toast, then Auntie Sanni's exquisite apple meringues – she made them herself. Afterwards there was cheese and Samuel brought round a perfect port – 'With Colonel Sahib's compliments.'

———

'Coffee served on the veranda, Sahib.' Deep in talk they had not been conscious that, though the other waiters had gone, Samuel was still there.

'I'm sorry, Samuel,' said Michael.

'Sahib is welcome.'

Nor did they want coffee. 'I think,' said Inspector Dutta, 'I shall take a stroll in the garden and go to bed.'

'What a good idea.'

They walked in silence across the lawn, avoiding the beach. Michael was still flying but not in an aeroplane. The surf thundered even in this peaceful garden, full of shadows with only gleams of light from the house. From a bush near the steps there was a scent of such sweetness and strength that it wafted far over the lawn. He could see its small white flowers and stopped. 'Isn't that . . .?'

'*Raht ki rani*,' said the Inspector.

'Queen of the Night. Yes, I remember.'

'They say its perfume is so strong it can make you giddy.'

'I am giddy.'

But the Inspector was not listening. He sighed. 'It is on nights like this that I miss my wife,' and, as Michael was silent, he asked, 'Michael, have you a wife?'

'No, thank you. I am very well arranged as I am.'

'Poor Michael! Good night.'

On impulse Michael went to have a last look at the Shiva, and this time it was he who made Auntie Sanni jump. She was in her dressing gown, standing below the niche where the small lamp burned. He saw that her lips were moving, her eyes rapt, although she put out a hand to stay him. When she had finished, she turned to him and smiled. 'I am making my night prayer.'

'To Shiva?' He could not help being slightly shocked: he had taken it for granted that she was a Christian until, once again, as if she had divined his thinking she said, 'Why do religions feel they must have edges? To me they are all one, as in this house. Our Goanese cook and Samuel and Hannah are Catholics.'

'As Hannah told me. She said Thomist Christian.'

'She would. St Thomas is supposed to have come to Madras. She is very devoted, but works happily with all the others. Colonel McIndoe's personal valet is Buddhist, as are the houseboys. Or perhaps they are Hindu – they come from Nepal. The table servants are Muslims, our gardeners Brahmins, the highest Hindu caste of all, and the sweepers, men and women, are Hindus too but rank so low they have no caste at all. They are outcasts and called "untouchables" yet they all work together happily at Patna Hall.'

'And revere the Nataraja.'

'Yes.'

'But this one? It doesn't rival the true one for beauty and feeling. Auntie Sanni, I went to see it in London.'

'So,' she said, 'to you this is not the same?'

'Not quite. This is a wonderful copy made by a craftsman who has a touch of the artist, but I can't help thinking of that complete artist who carved the other so long ago. The power . . .'

'Shiva's power.'

Michael's instinct made a sudden leap. 'Auntie Sanni, I think you have known about the changeover all the time.'

Auntie Sanni looked at him severely. 'I am not saying anything. Good night.'

—◁▷—

Michael felt he owed himself a morning on the beach and, after a Patna Hall English breakfast – bacon and egg with mushrooms, toast, home-made marmalade and coffee – he changed into his trunks and a beach-robe that he found in his cupboard with a wide towel. He followed the stepping stones across the white sands, already warm with sun, until he came to the foreshore strewn with shells and flotsam brought in by long ripples from the waves. Crabs scurried across it, there was an occasional starfish and blue jellyfish. All along was the barrier of tossing white, higher than his head, as the waves swept in, rearing up before crashing down; he had not realized last night quite how gigantic they were. Beyond them the open sea was calm and azure blue.

Patna Hall's beach was forbidden to the local fishermen and had its own security guards in Thambi and his assistant Moses.

'Ours is not a gentle sea,' Auntie Sanni had told Michael, as she told all her guests, when she saw him in his bathrobe. She always said, 'Please remember it is dangerous to go in alone to bathe, even for strong swimmers. You must take a guard.'

Michael went in with Thambi, who brought him one of the wicker helmets he had been carrying last night and helped him to adjust it tightly. Michael felt the pointed peak and knew how strong it was. Thambi also had a light surfboard so that Michael, having dived through the surf, could ride in on the height and speed of the wave, Thambi swimming alongside.

Once Michael went down to the seabed, he would have felt the full thud of the wave had he not been wearing the helmet but its peak pierced the water and he was borne up again, in the exultation of riding to be tumbled over and over on to the open sand.

Afterwards, peacefully exhausted, he lay on his towel in the sun and Thambi brought a beach umbrella to shade his head. I must make plans, he thought, but the peace, with the light breeze bringing not fragrance as it had last night but sunshine and saltiness, began to overtake him and he felt sleep steal over him. After all, he had been working with Mr Bhatacharya and Walter up to the last moment, then had had the long flight. There had been, too, this strange inner excitement and an elation he could not suppress. All this is quite normal, he told himself. If you work in law you go anywhere, anytime. Yet it still felt anything but normal. You must let go, he told himself.

'You didn't come out here to let go,' an inner voice seemed to say.

Only for an hour or two, he pleaded, but before anything more could be said, he was asleep.

Thambi shook him respectfully. 'Sahib. I think time to wake up. Twelve o'clock. Tiffin – lunch served soon.'

Still half asleep, Michael put on his robe and went up to the house. Lady Fisher, on the veranda, was quietly sewing – he had seen her embroidery last night. He went round to the portico, thinking he would go in by the hall, and his sleepiness was immediately banished.

A coach was standing there; houseboys were unloading suitcases and grips while, from the hall, came a hubbub of voices, chattering, laughing, exclaiming. The cultural ladies – cultural group! He almost said it aloud.

He dodged back into the garden, up the veranda steps – not disturbing Lady Fisher – but there was a dilemma. To reach the stairs and get to his room there was no other way than up the staircase from the hall, and it was crowded with men and women, still in their travelling clothes and carrying their impedimenta: handbags, shoulder-bags full of books, notebooks, papers and maps; cameras, binoculars, radios; some of the older people had walking sticks. Kanu, full of importance, had a queue for registering, a pile of passports, and was handing out keys.

Professor Ellen was in the midst of it, introducing the group to Auntie Sanni one by one, with a few married pairs, always breaking off to produce others: 'Mr and Mrs Horne, Dr Sidney Duncan and Miss

Susan Carmichael' – Not married, thought Michael – 'Madame Duvivier who joined us from Paris,' *soignée*, elegant. 'Ian Macpherson, and you must meet our Chinese student, Ansie Lee. Ansie, where are you? Ansie.'

One young woman had not waited but introduced herself: 'I'm Marcia Barclay, my husband Eric. We work at Sussex University. I'm so glad we came. Ellen has told us so much about you. Your marvellous mulligatawny soup.'

'Marcia!' Her unmistakably English husband tried to curb her.

'Well, I'm starving. Could we be having it for lunch?'

Auntie Sanni had been caught by somebody else but, 'Mulligatawny on lunch menu' – Samuel had come, in full regalia, to help receive the group, while Hannah was on the stairs, which was just as well. Already there was a complaint.

'I hope I'm on the first floor,' wailed a voice. 'It seems there is no lift.' It was one of the more elderly ladies, cross-looking. 'A hotel with no lift!'

'Memsahib is on first floor.' Hannah had immediately come down. 'Stairs easy. See, Hannah help you.'

Pillars of the house, Michael remembered Auntie Sanni saying, but already the group were calling the woman Mrs Moaner. 'There's one on every tour.' Professor Ellen was back.

Michael tried to flatten himself against the wall. He knew Auntie Sanni had seen him, but she had a policy at Patna Hall that one guest should never be introduced to another unless both wanted it. Professor Ellen had no such restrictions: 'Oh, Michael, there you are. Come and meet Mark and Millicent Erle. They're so interested in—' but she broke off to speak to another guest and Michael never learned what Mark and Millicent were interested in, nor when she came back with a younger woman, 'Ann, meet Mr Dean. Michael, Ann does all our—' did he discover what Ann did.

As Lady Fisher had said, there were plenty of young, standing a little apart; they wore jeans and T-shirts, their hair cropped short or for the girls let loose and streaming. One large boy had his tied in a pony-tail and wore an ear-ring. A girl, obviously waiting to go upstairs, still carried her rucksack on her back. Independent, that one, thought Michael.

Professor Ellen came over with especial quickness to introduce them. 'Maria, Jacky, Di, Marilyn, Morgan, Tom.' The names swirled round Michael. 'Duke, Charlie.'

'Hello. How do you do?' That was a girl, while the young man called Duke asked, 'You here for the archaeology, like us?'

'I wish I were,' said Michael, 'but no, I'm on other business.'

Duke was well-mannered and did not ask further

questions. 'This seems like a nice place,' he had begun instead, when Auntie Sanni came over to them.

'Wouldn't it be nice if you found your rooms?' Half the crowd had already gone. 'I expect you want to wash and then come down to our veranda bar and have a cool drink.'

'It sounds heavenly,' cried Marcia Barclay, 'and then lunch, and you promised us mulligatawny.'

'Marcia!' But Samuel made her a small bow. 'Memsahib quite right. One of Patna Hall's famous soups. Wait till you taste, Sahib,' he said to Michael, but Michael was not listening. He was looking beyond them. 'I saw her,' he always said afterwards, 'I can never forget it.' A young woman, not talking but leaning on the reception counter. There was a coolness about her as she looked on at the flock she had brought so far, watching with a gentle tolerance as if they were, indeed, a flock and she their shepherd.

Michael, though, was surprised at himself because she was dressed in a way that usually would have alienated him at once: an Edwardian-length, draggle-tailed black cotton skirt and a white muslin blouse with a frilled neckline. Nothing more unsuitable for travelling could be imagined; it seemed almost wilful. Her dark hair was up, with rat-tails, which he particularly abhorred, but perhaps it was the poise of her head, proud, the grace with which she leaned on the counter. Forgetting his bathrobe and skilfully avoiding Professor Ellen, he wove his way through the remaining crowd, who were moving towards the stairs. 'Good morning.'

Her gaze immediately came to him. Her eyes were blue – but the dark blue of sapphires. They lit up when she saw him; evidently she approved. 'Hello, I'm Artemis.'

'I knew that the moment I saw you. I'm Michael.'

'Ellen told me the lawyer was coming for the defence but you're too young to be a lawyer. We all thought he would have spectacles and be cagy and wise.'

'I think I'm very wise. I saw you across the room and came straight to you.' But Professor Ellen had come too. 'I see you've found each other, but I must help Auntie Sanni.'

Auntie Sanni was talking to the young people, who were the last to be shown upstairs. 'I hope you won't mind sleeping in Paradise,' she said. 'That's what we call a line of rooms on the roof, simple and small like cells.' She did not tell them that, in Patna Hall's grander days, they had been kept for the ladies' maids, valets and chauffeurs who came with Europeans, Americans, ambassadors or merchant princes.

'Yes, sleep in Paradise,' Artemis called. 'Up there you are almost in the sky. You can see this whole world, land and sea, and at night you will be close to the stars. If any of you don't want to sleep there I will.'

'No, dear, you won't.' Professor Ellen had drawn her aside but although she whispered, Michael could hear every word. 'Artemis dear, if you do that, fraternize completely, you won't keep your authority.' To Michael she explained, 'Artemis Knox, I hope, is going to succeed me. You can't imagine what she has done for us, or how serious she is, coming every year for the last five, the only person I have ever had who hired a car and went into the hills on her own. She has even learned Telegu, and last year she brought a film unit with lights and camera, which showed us so much we didn't know about the cave paintings.'

But Artemis was still rebellious. 'I hate authority.'

'All the same, you'll find it your greatest asset.'

'I know, and I use it all the time.' Artemis was suddenly wistful. 'That's what makes me so sad. Before I had it — or have I always had it? — I was free.' She looked so forlorn that Michael felt a strange pull.

Is that what they call heart-strings? he wondered. He had not known he had any — his affairs had always been light-hearted. And to feel it so quickly? It isn't possible. But the answer was that he did feel it. He put out a hand to touch her, but she had darted across the hall — empty now that the young people had gone upstairs — and she was hugging Auntie Sanni. 'At last I have a chance to kiss you. Oh, it's so good to be back!' She was smiling and there was a dimple on each cheek.

The dimples finished Michael.

———

When he came down, changed for lunch, he found that Auntie Sanni had been right: the veranda, which had been so quiet, was filled to overflowing with people, voices, chatter and laughter, as the hall had been. She had Mark and Millicent with her on her throne and seemed to have taken over the Chinese Ansie; the other young people had carried their drinks to the garden steps, but most were gathered round the bar where Kanu, in his striped jacket, was a little repressed by Colonel McIndoe helping him; it was he who had suggested a John Collins, gin and ginger beer taken long with plenty of ice. 'I expect you've been warned about ice in India. It's often made with water that hasn't been boiled, but our butler, Samuel, sees to that himself so you're safe.' Some had mango juice or iced tea. Kanu was further depressed by being asked if he could make mint julep, of which he had never heard, and to his chagrin he had to consult Samuel. Michael took up a position by the bar where he could listen and watch while Professor Ellen went from one cluster to another, asking if they had settled in.

'Indeed we have,' said Marcia, 'it's lovely.' Her Eric was drinking with the other men so she could be as exuberant as she chose: no one would have believed she was a serious archaeologist.

The group had landed in Delhi, gone to Calcutta and Dacca. 'So we've had hotels, and after that Uberoi chain, all exactly alike, I never expected anything like this. Sheer bliss.'

There was an echo of agreement until, 'Bliss? You call it bliss.' It was Mrs Moaner. 'I certainly didn't expect anything like this – no telephone in the room, no television or room service. That nice young man at the desk says that this Miss Sanni, as we are expected to call her, refuses to modernize.'

'Oh, come,' said Artemis, who had slipped in quietly. 'Patna Hall has air-conditioning and electricity.'

Michael was glad to see she had changed into a sun-dress with a poppy red skirt and brief bodice; its white straps over her shoulders and across her bare back showed off her skin – surprisingly not sunburned but as petal fine as Lady Fisher's. It had a glow he had not seen in girls he had met in London. I suppose it's energy and health. She wore the lightest of sandals and her hair was tied with a red chiffon scarf. She doesn't have to look a mess, thought Michael, with relief.

Though the veranda was in shade, the air was warm and balmy, and the sunlight from outside made patterns on the floor. The garden basked in midday brightness but a soft breeze brought the fragrance of flowers. There was a chatter of parakeets – their bright green and red could be seen in the trees – the harsh caw of crows, and mynah birds, brown with orange beaks, hopped on the floor looking for the crumbs Marcia threw for them. Michael had never felt more content and peaceful.

There's something about this place and about that girl . . . he thought, but Mrs Moaner was grizzling on. 'And what about the bathroom?' she demanded. He could understand that, particularly to an American, Patna Hall's plumbing arrangements were primitive. 'Never did I think I should have to sit on a stool in a little room divided by a kerb, with one tap, and *that's* cold, and pour water over me with an outsize zinc mug.'

'Lovely warm water, just as you want it, plenty of it, standing in *gharras*, those big earthenware pots freshly filled ready for you.' Artemis tried to soothe her.

'And should we not, if we come to a country, do as they do?' asked Madame Duvivier.

'And isn't it part of the fun?' asked Dora, a small twinkling brunette who sat on one of the wicker couches with her Jamaican friend, Kate.

'It's this sort of fun that makes this place so different.' Marcia grew more enthusiastic every minute.

'Fun! Downright cheating and not even hygienic.'

Artemis lost patience. 'It's odd you should say

72

that, when the Indians think it is we who are unhygienic in having a bath, lying in the water of our own dirt.'

'*Dirt!*' Mrs Moaner was truly shocked. 'How dare they? I've never been dirty in my life. Oh, I wish I'd never come.'

'We can easily fly you back tomorrow if you like,' said cruel Artemis.

At that moment, fortunately, Samuel sounded the gong.

'Whoops! Mulligatawny soup,' cried Marcia, as they all sprang to their feet, but now Michael saw a completely different Artemis.

She had gone to Mrs Moaner. 'Come,' she said, with all her charm. 'I'm sure you'll feel much happier when you've had some lunch. The food here is truly good. Oh! You haven't finished your drink. Never mind. Take it with you. I'll bring it. Let me help you up.' And Mrs Moaner went with her, smiling.

'You see? She can manage them.' Professor Ellen was at his elbow.

'Sure as God made little green apples.' Her earnestness made Michael flippant.

'There's nothing green about Artemis,' she said at once.

The group had two long tables. Professor Ellen was at the head of one. She tinkled a knife against a tumbler to make an announcement. 'This afternoon you will probably like to rest or go on the beach.

This evening Miss Sanni is kindly giving a reception and supper to welcome us.' Artemis was at the head of the other table; again, she had that look of authority though she laughed and talked. Michael found himself watching her all through luncheon while he carried on an absent-minded conversation with Inspector Dutta, who said, at last, 'Michael, you are not listening to me at all!'

'I'm sorry, Hem.'

'I am asking if you would like to come with me this afternoon to the village and bazaar?'

Michael was jerked back to his own world.

'If you don't want to come, never mind.'

'But I do, of course I do, especially as I must as soon as possible. Thank you, Hem.'

<hr />

'I long to see a bazaar again,' said Michael, as they set out. Inspector Dutta had two of his men with him, a sergeant from his home town, who spoke Hindi, and a young trainee who spoke Telegu, which was why he was given this opportunity. Both knew English. In the garden Auntie Sanni had turned a hut into an office for them; she did not want police work in the house.

Now they went out past Patna Hall's big double gates and its lodge where Thambi lived. His handsome, big-breasted young wife, Shyama, was supposed to be the gatekeeper but as they were always kept open she had nothing to do and did nothing but wash her hair, spreading it on her shoulders to dry as she lazed in the sun. If Thambi happened to come home – he did the shopping and cooking – he would pick up a tress, run it through his fingers and kiss it.

At dusk, though, Shyama would come out and light the little oil lamp below the sacred small *tulsi* tree they kept in their courtyard. When the flame was steady, she would blow on a big conch shell, 'Ulla-la, ulla-la, ullah.' To Thambi it was a call home.

'Well, Shyama is very lovely,' said Auntie Sanni. 'Plump and sweet.'

Michael thought that too when, although she had hidden her face in her sari, she opened it a little to smile at him.

'When I was a child,' Michael told the Inspector – and he felt he was a child again – 'I was not supposed to go into the bazaar alone, but I got over the wall of our garden and went wandering.'

'Has it changed very much?'

'Not really, except for all the plastic, plastic everything. *Gharras*, water pots, plates. They used to use banana leaves but now plastic tumblers, toys, even bangles.'

Plastic and electricity – usually a single bulb hanging on a cord – and radios blaring, yet the bazaar had not changed. There were still the lines of shanty shops, all open booths showing their wares: sacks of grain or rice, vegetables piled high or floating in water; saris hung up or carefully folded on shelves; baby jackets on tiny hangers, flat as paper. There were cookshops where samosas and puris sizzled in open pans, and the smell of hot mustard oil mingled with the stench of urine from the gutter. A barber was shaving his client in the open while a letter writer had his floor desk on the pavement, his paper, ink and stamps ready. There were the inevitable crows with their harsh voices, pigeons, mynah birds, some in cages, and nanny goats, with their udders shut away from their kids in muslin bags. There was even a sacred bull, helping itself unhindered from a grain bag or vegetable stall; its hump was covered by a cap worked with beads. And there were, of course, the people, walkers, shoppers, children running loose, babies crawling and, in the road, bicycle rickshaws, their hoods patterned with flowers, their bells ringing, and a swarm of small black-and-yellow three-wheeled taxis hooting incessantly. 'Those are new,' said Michael. 'I've never seen them before, but I'm back.'

They came to a kite shop that could have been the one where he had bought his kites, made of the thinnest paper in pink, green, red, white stretched on the lightest cross-bars of bamboo. He seemed to feel the wickerwork spool turning as he flew them. 'We used to pass our thread through a mixture of ground glass and glue so that it would cut.'

'So did we,' said Inspector Dutta.

'Then challenge another kite by dipping ours. If

it dipped back we crossed strings, which was where the skill showed. I was a mighty kite fighter.'

'So was I.'

Michael cajoled him, 'Hem, let's forget about the case, fit ourselves out and go down to the beach for a kite fight.'

His companion looked at him severely. This was another side of the genial Inspector Dutta. 'Mr Dean, we are searching the bazaar, not playing but looking for the slightest clue. Also I have my sergeant with me. What would he think? And the trainee, who is here to learn. It seems you, too, need to learn.'

Still Michael found it difficult to pay attention. The front of the money-changer's jewellery shop had bars across it, with the man sitting behind them on a red cushion quilted with black and white flowers. Although this was South India, Michael knew he was from Marwar in Rajasthan: the Marwaris were renowned as businessmen and financiers. He had a small black cap on his head and many ledgers in front of him.

There was apparently nothing in his shop but a safe, a pair of scales and a table a few inches high on which he displayed the items that he brought out from the safe. In India jewellery is sold by weight and often made of silver threads, woven into patterns and flowers. While Inspector Dutta talked to the man, Michael bought a pair of his filigree silver ear-rings for Honor.

Then he saw a small temple and went across to it. The outside walls and floors were tessellated with broken china, countless pieces set in concrete. Its pointed roof was covered in beaten-out kerosene tins which shone silver in the sun, but the painted plaster gods of his childhood had been replaced by two large, jointed Western dolls. They were dressed in gaudy muslin, tinsel and paper flowers, but Michael knew that the priest put them to bed every night, got them up in the morning. 'Hindus worship round the clock,' he had told Honor, and, true, before these doll-gods was a low table with offerings of sweets and flowers. As he watched, a woman came to pray; on the brass tray she put a little powdered sugar making with her thumb a pattern on it for luck. 'But what a shame to have those dolls,' Michael said to Inspector Dutta. 'They used to have wonderful home-made images.'

'They still do,' said the Inspector. 'You must come and meet Veeranna, the potter. His name means "one who is brave and good in his work", which he is. A fine modeller.'

Michael had already smelt the kiln. 'That smell makes me remember that every village has a potter.'

'Often more than one, but for how long can they last now that we have plastics? Of course, plastics are far more sensible.'

'Ugh!'

The Inspector laughed. 'You can cheer up. We still need potters. Festival images cannot be made of plastic because at the end of their *puja* or feast they are taken to the nearest water − here it is the sea − and they are immersed and have to disintegrate. Veeranna is busy now because the feast of Vinayak Chauthuri is near, when Ganesh, the elephant-headed god, is worshipped. Most of the time he finds it hard to make a living out of clay but, being gifted, he has been trying to do metal work. I believe he went on a course to learn.'

The potter's workshop was away from the village. 'But villagers, even though they are converted to plastic, revere their potter if he is an image-maker as well,' Inspector Dutta told Michael, 'because it seems to them that out of the air, or earth because he works in clay, he can conjure up any god they need, from the little household gods kept in a house's prayer corner, to the life-size ones that are the central figures in a feast when they stand in a *pandal*, a sort of arbour, in the village square or street to be worshipped. Any god or goddess. The people think that marvellous. Veeranna, though, is not sociable, never married and lives a lonely life, immersed in his work.'

His house had the same earthen-clay walls and floors, the same thatched roof as any in the village but it was bigger, having two rooms and a more spacious courtyard shaded by trees. The larger room was for living as well as work, with an open fire for cooking in one corner, a low wooden bed held together by a web of strings, its quilts tidily rolled up.

Veeranna evidently believed in order: lines of clay bowls, some little and others as big as *gharras*, stood in the courtyard, largely unsold, but the centre of the room was taken up by his wooden wheel which he spun while sitting on the floor. Beside it was a hole dug wide in which he mixed his clay.

The kiln was outside but so near the threshold that the room's upper walls and inside roof were blackened by the fumes. 'He lights the kiln with coal and cakes of cow dung, which he collects and dries in pats on the house wall outside. But see,' said Inspector Dutta, 'those are jars of glazing made out of local rock, powdered and mixed with soda ash.' Shelves propped on bricks held 'Pigments of all colours,' said the Inspector, 'especially gilt. He has to paint his images.' On another, wider, shelf were the properties needed for the gods: musical instruments – flutes and, especially, little hand drums – swords, arrows, beads, even a stuffed snake or two, crowns, jewellery, bolts of gauze cloth, some patterned with gold stars or silver crescent moons, or woven with gold thread and with gold borders.

'He must have a good trade,' said Michael.

'He says, enough.'

When they had come in – without knocking, Michael noticed – Veeranna had been sitting on the floor painting in the finishing touches of gilt on the crown of a Ganesh, already complete, even to his short gleaming tusks. For a moment the potter did not lay down his paintbrush, then abandoned it and stood up reluctantly, salaaming.

Veeranna was almost as big as Thambi but modelled more finely. As if he had modelled himself, thought Michael, who looked particularly at his hands, large, long and strong-fingered, the thumbs spatulate and bent wide, almost double-jointed. As he faced the policemen, his hands were never still – Nervous, thought Michael. Unlike Thambi's golden brown skin, Veeranna's was as dark as only a Dravidian's can be: when he dived into the room's shadows – he seemed to think it necessary to show Michael this or that piece of pottery – he almost disappeared and only the whites of his eyes glinted. When he stood in the light, Michael saw that the irises were brown not black as he had expected, and that Veeranna had unusually long lashes. He is proud and sensitive, thought Michael, yet childlike in the way he treats me, this stranger sahib, even though he was obviously frightened by the policemen: 'Police mean trouble.' Michael could have said it for him.

They went into the inner room. 'This is where Veeranna says he will do the metal work that so inspires him.' But the room had nothing in it except a wooden turntable and a bright neon light on the ceiling.

'Nothing else?' Michael was disappointed.

'I expect it is as far as he has got,' said the Inspector. 'The tools are most expensive but Veeranna

is determined. I am sure he will get them in time.'
But now Veeranna was beckoning.

'He says he have something to show Sahib,' the
young trainee told them.

As they watched, Veeranna went to a wall where
finished images stood. Because of the coming feast,
most were of Ganesh, but one figure, taller than the
others, was carefully swathed in muslin and, with
something like triumph, Veeranna took off the cover-
ings, lifted it and put it down before Michael, who
was astounded. He whispered, 'Saraswati.'

'Yes. Goddess of all learning.' Inspector Dutta was
intent on his information.

'Goddess of pen and ink,' Michael remembered,
'and music too, of course. She always holds a *vina*.
On her *puja* day I remember they used to set up a
pandal for her in the street and the students and poets,
and schoolchildren, used to bring their books, manu-
scripts and instruments and lay them at her feet. I
always thought she was beautiful, but this is lovely.
Tell him so,' he told the young trainee. Veeranna
had given her a gauze sari, patterned with little gold
stars, a crescent moon in her hair, even the holy little
red henna spot that marks devoted women's fore-
heads. Her smile was so gracious she seemed alive. In
English so quick that neither of the young policemen
could follow it, Michael said in the Inspector's ear,
'Don't you think Veeranna could have made the new
Shiva?'

Inspector Dutta gave a loud guffaw. 'Dear Michael, how you do get carried away! As I have said, Veeranna is a good craftsman but don't forget the Shiva is bronze and he has only just started working in metal – if he has. That needed an artist, someone approaching that old master sculptor. No village potter could possibly have made it.' As Veeranna was standing looking puzzled, the Inspector said to the young trainee, 'Translate for him.'

Veeranna listened, said nothing, only picked up the Saraswati to put her away, but Michael had seen a gleam of resentment in his eyes.

――◆――

When they came back to Patna Hall the sun was still hot. 'I think I'll go in for a dip,' said Michael. 'I'll fetch my things.'

He came back to find Inspector Dutta at the head of the beach watching Artemis: she was standing at the top of the high diving board built far out into the bay with the surf sending up a turbulence of white against it. In her wicker helmet and turquoise bikini, she was wet and her body glistened. She stood taut, her hands held high and joined ready. Thambi was beside her but not touching her as they dived, she in a perfect curve far out beyond the waves, swimming ahead of him. They were clapping her on the beach as Inspector Dutta said, 'Is there anything that young woman cannot do?'

Then, unexpectedly, 'I'm glad I haven't got her for a wife.'

Michael did not answer; he was too intent. She went down – he caught his breath – but came up and rode in on the surf, Thambi holding her on a gigantic wave that, as it fell, rolled them far up the shore, spreading ripples round them as they lay panting but laughing until Artemis staggered up the sand and fell on her swimming towel, spread ready.

'She best of all,' Thambi told Michael, who had dared to walk over.

'Thambi says that to everyone,' said Artemis. 'Don't you, Thambi?'

'This time true.' Thambi laughed. 'Sahib want to go in?'

'He can't. He's going to talk to me,' and Artemis patted the sand beside her. 'Come on, sit down,' and as Michael obeyed, 'Tell me something nice and nothing to do with people. People, people, people!' She was vehement. 'Tell me something innocent as if we were children.'

Sitting on the warm sand, scooping it up to let it trickle through his fingers, by some magic Michael was inspired to begin:

'And then with hat and ball and hoop go playing
in parks where the bright colours softly fade,
brushing against the grown-ups without staying
when ball or hoop their alien walks invade . . .

84

And hours on end by the grey pond-side kneeling
with little sailing-boat and elbows bare;
forgetting it, because one like it's stealing
below the ripples, but with sails more fair;
and, having still to spare, to share some feeling
with the small face caught sight of there:-
Childhood! winged likeness half-guessed at, wheeling,
oh, where, oh, where?'

Artemis turned on her side and looked at him. 'I didn't know brilliant young men could quote poetry.'

'I'm not brilliant.'

'Auntie Sanni says you are and she knows.' The teasing stopped. 'Perhaps knows too much,' she said. For a moment she turned away, then back to look at him again. 'Do you write poems, Michael?'

'I have.'

'Say one.' It was a command, and something in Michael told him to rebel.

'No, thank you!' he said, got up and walked away.

─── ◆ ───

Artemis did not come for drinks or dinner: she was busy helping to arrange the drawing room–ballroom for Auntie Sanni and the Colonel's supper reception. Samuel was there too, and the dining room was almost empty. Only the Fishers, Inspector Dutta and

Michael were having dinner, waited on by the head waiter. Professor Ellen had a bad headache so that after dinner the four of them were alone on the veranda while from the ballroom they could hear music.

Michael showed Lady Fisher the ear-rings he had bought for Honor. 'These are really good ones,' said Lady Fisher, 'beautiful. It's amazing what you can find in a village bazaar.'

This led to talk of Honor. 'To us, she's just a young girl,' said Sir John. 'We can hardly believe she's a QC.'

'What is that?' asked Inspector Dutta.

'Queen's Counsel. A very senior barrister. Apparently in her year there were over five hundred applicants and perhaps seventy were admitted. There's a huge waiting list.'

'Of whom only eight were women,' said Lady Fisher.

'Honor has been a QC for five years which, of course, has led to her high status,' and Sir John explained to Inspector Dutta, 'It's all deeply traditional. As a QC, in court you have to wear a full-bottomed wig, gloves, buckled shoes and the traditional black silk gown, which is why it's called taking silk.'

'Taking silk. I like that,' said Inspector Dutta.

Professor Ellen came down: 'To have a little fresh air, and a brandy if I may?' she asked Sir John. The music had changed, dancing had begun. 'I find this the hardest work of all.' She had collapsed into a chair. 'Thank God for Artemis but I shall have to go in soon.'

'And I have just come out.' Auntie Sanni had appeared. 'A brandy for me too, please, John. Ellen, you look very pale.'

'I feel it, but Artemis is there.'

'It seems strange,' said Michael, 'noisy dancing in a room that has a shrine in it.'

'They have dancing girls in temples,' Sir John pointed out.

'But not for this sort of dancing.'

'That reminds me.' Inspector Dutta's thoughts were never far from his work. 'Professor Webster, in your experience, since Henry Bertram's time, did the Nataraja ever go out of the house?'

'Yes. I'd been worried about it. The sea air and saltiness were beginning to erode it. Of course, it should have been kept under glass.'

'Under glass!' Auntie Sanni was indignant. 'That would have defeated its purpose.'

'You see?' Professor Ellen shrugged. 'But Artemis is bolder than I. In her explorations she had come to know a renowned old sculptor, Sri Satya Narayana, who specialized in antiques. He himself used the centuries-old ancient methods, carving in wax. The season before last, Artemis had arranged not to fly home but to spend the summer, the hot weather, researching in Kashmir, and offered to take the Shiva to Sri Narayana on her way there, picking it up on her way back.'

'She went by car?'

'Yes,' Auntie Sanni confirmed.

'With an escort, I hope?'

'Escort? What escort?'

'The Shiva is very valuable, Miss Sanni.'

'Well, Artemis just took it but it was no good. When she got to Sri Narayana's house-studio to collect the Nataraja on her way back, she found he had died two months before without touching it so she brought it back.'

'And you are sure, Professor, that it was the same?'

'Of course it was, there was no mistaking it, and that was last year. It was only this year that I knew at once that what we now have is a fake.'

'Long after Miss Artemis brought it back?'

'Yes.' Professor Ellen was firm.

'Well, if you'll excuse me I'll go up. I want to write to Honor,' Michael told the Fishers.

He could hear Indian music now. What will Mrs Moaner have to say about that, he wondered. For him it conjured up the magic of Veeranna's Saraswati and the *vina* in her hand. The hall, though, was deserted until the drawing-room door opened and Artemis came out, closing it quickly behind her.

She was dressed in what Michael guessed she had adopted as her uniform. Another long black skirt and white frilled blouse, but these were fresh and clean, while her hair was up in a knot tied with another red chiffon scarf. She looked what she was, a leader, but she leaned back against the door and gave a wide yawn.

'Tired?' Michael's voice was tender.

'Michael!' At once she was poised again, as she said, 'You were so cross on the beach I thought you would never speak to me again.'

'Silly! You know I'll always want to speak to you, Artemis . . .'

He had come closer but before he could touch her she was gone – back to the other side of the door.

———

'Today is your day for the Sun Temple at Konak.' Although it was early, Sir John was up and had found Professor Ellen with her list waiting for the group to come downstairs.

'Yes,' she said, 'we're just getting ready.' The coach was waiting under the portico as the group gathered, carrying their usual paraphernalia. Samuel was taking on board freezer bags of iced mineral water, orange juice, biscuits and tea-making things.

'It's a long way,' said Sir John. 'They only arrived yesterday and I see Artemis is giving a lecture tonight.'

'Yes, on the sculptures. She really has become an expert.'

'I'm sure, but, my dear, how you do drive them.'

'That's what they came for. They wouldn't be satisfied with anything less.'

'I don't know if I want to go or not.' Mrs Moaner had come downstairs with Hannah.

'Memsahib try,' Hannah encouraged. 'I'm sure if you get tired Professor Miss Sahib send you back by car.'

'They say it's dreadfully erotic.'

'That's why I want to go.'

Duke's eyes sparkled, but Madame Duvivier said, perhaps in gentle rebuke, 'It's the beauty and majesty we go to see.'

'Michael.' He had just appeared and Professor Ellen came eagerly up to him. 'Why don't you come too? It's such a chance.'

'I'm afraid there are things I have to do.' He did not want to hurt her feelings but, as he told Lady Fisher when the coach had left, 'If I can get to Konak I shall go by myself, not in a group with a guided tour.'

'You're right,' said Lady Fisher. 'It's truly the most beautiful temple in the world, built like a vast stone chariot with huge carved wheels and drawn by gigantic stone horses that seem alive. No one has ever fathomed how men — ants by comparison — got the great slabs of stone in place. To see its full beauty you need to be there at the moment when the risen sun touches the entrance, which is guarded by two stone lions crushing elephants, where Surya the sun god sits on his charger as if in welcome. His face has a wonderfully beneficent smile for all who come to pay tribute at his temple. I can't tell you how beautiful it is but you must get up at three or four in the morning. We always did, didn't we, John?'

In her own quiet way Lady Fisher knew even more about this vast country than Artemis.

Artemis! Be sensible, Michael had told himself that very morning. She has things to do and you have things to do, so get on with it.

Samuel had given him a note. It was from Inspector Dutta.

Shall be away for about twenty-four hours.
Colonel McIndoe has my telephone number but
I shall be moving about. Think I am on to
something.

So am I, thought Michael.

He had not forgotten that gleam of resentment in Veeranna's eyes and knew he had to go and see him – with someone to translate.

❧

Instinctively, he did not take Thambi – he was too senior – so, 'Moses,' he said, 'I want to explore the village but I don't speak Telegu and you speak good English.' A little flattery, he had learned, goes a long way. 'Will you come with me?'

'I very pleased, Sahib. I not needed here this morning.'

Quiet lay over Patna Hall. Auntie Sanni and the Colonel were busy at their desks; Sir John had gone for a quiet stroll along the beach; Lady Fisher was, as usual, on the veranda. There was, of course, no sign of Inspector Dutta, nor had he been at breakfast.

'I come now,' said Moses.

Michael and he set out. As they walked through the gates, Michael smiled again at Shyama, who was in the courtyard sitting on a rush mat dreamily shifting chillies, which were turning scarlet in the sun. She could not hide her face in her sari, which was hanging down her back, leaving her brief bodice and bare midriff showing plump, but this time she smiled back boldly. Out of respect for Thambi, Moses ignored her.

There was a telephone call for Michael. It came to Colonel McIndoe's office – to Kanu's indignation the Colonel did not allow direct calls to reception. Now he pressed a buzzer which Samuel, who was nearest, answered. 'Fetch Dean Sahib. There is a call for him. It's from London so be quick.'

Michael was not in his room, or on the veranda.

Samuel sent a boy running to the beach but he was not on the beach. It seemed he was out with Moses. Why Moses, Samuel wondered. Michael was usually with Thambi. After a moment he went to the gatehouse. 'The young English sahib,' he asked Shyama in Telegu – she was too indolent to pick up even a few words of English – 'did he go out?'

'Yes,' whispered Shyama. She was in awe of Samuel, who clicked his tongue in annoyance.

The Colonel was irritated, too. 'Think of the expense. Why didn't they send a fax?' But Samuel's annoyance was not at the telephone call: he had a deeper dismay.

'The young sahib. Was he alone?' he asked Shyama.

'No. With Moses.'

Now Samuel was truly alarmed.

<hr />

'What I really want,' Michael told Moses, 'is to go and see the potter.'

'Him Veeranna.'

'I know.'

'Very good potter. Most clever. He make beautiful god and goddess.'

'I know.'

Veeranna was making one now, working on still another Ganesh whose elephant trunk was almost completed. He was absorbed, a lump of clay in his left hand, which he took, scrap by scrap, working it in with his thumb. He did not notice them until Moses touched his shoulder, almost reverently, but as soon as he saw Michael he was up, letting the clay fall back into the hole on the floor.

Copying Inspector Dutta, Michael said, 'Veeranna *bhai*,' and made a *namaskar*, his hands held together finger to finger in the Indian greeting he had learned as a little boy. 'Tell him, Moses, the Ganesh will be very good.'

Veeranna's face cleared as Moses translated and he returned the greeting.

'Ask him if he has ever made a god in metal.'

There was quite a conversation during which Veeranna was obviously proud. 'Him say yes. He take many lessons . . .'

'Where?'

At that Veeranna withdrew. All Moses could get from him was, 'Far away.'

'Ask him for how long.'

More talk with Moses, then, 'He say two years. Not all the year. He go and come. He has his work here.'

Michael wasted no more time. 'Veeranna, you made the second Shiva Nataraja, didn't you?'

There was no need to translate. For a moment Veeranna shone. 'Sahib has eyes! *Ji hah!* Yes, I made him and fool all those clever sahibs.' Veeranna threw

94

back his head and laughed, a deep, throaty, delighted laugh.

Michael's instinct was to stop there – 'If only I had,' he said afterwards, 'but I felt bound to go on.'

'Veeranna *bhai*, you must have had help. Tell me . . .' But the delight was gone. Veeranna's face was stern, his lips shut tightly. 'Please tell.'

'I not tell,' and suddenly Veeranna turned to Moses with a torrent of words.

'He say he promise not tell. Sacred promise. If he break promise, Shiva punish him. Shiva punishment most terrible, Sahib.' Moses' eyes showed he had caught some of the terror and awe. 'Perhaps kill.'

'I not tell. Never. Go away.' Veeranna turned his back, sat down before his Ganesh on its plinth and picked up a ball of fresh clay.

Michael had given Moses a handsome tip, then shut himself in his room at the desk Auntie Sanni had sent up for him, his pad in front of him, as he went over the scene in the potter's house.

'Why? How? Who?'

How? Michael knew little about sculpture but enough to realize that, even granted much skill, such an exact replica could not have been made from memory or even photographs. Veeranna must have had the Nataraja before him every moment of his work, but if he had visited it in its niche, or openly borrowed it, everyone would have known.

Why? Michael felt sure he knew the answer to that. Veeranna, by bone, blood and brain, was an artist, and someone, though Michael could not imagine who, had given him the chance to show it – he a poor potter. He had been taught, elsewhere, thought Michael, been given tools. Someone had paid for all these.

That brought him to who, and here he was lost.

There was a knock at the door. It was Samuel. 'Dean Sahib, your call, in reception. It from London, so quick.'

It was a repeat call from Honor Wyatt. 'I could have faxed you but I wanted to hear your voice. Are you still alive and well?'

'Never been more alive and well.'

'Good. How's it going?'

'Inch by inch . . . at least I hope it is.'

— ⁓ —

'Of course I know,' said Hannah.

What had made Michael go to Hannah and not Samuel he could not say, even to himself. He found her on the top veranda, superintending the gardeners – sometimes with a sharp tongue – as they arranged vases of flowers they had brought freshly in; as each was finished a houseboy came and carried it away to a different room. Hannah would have broken off but

'Let them finish,' Michael said. 'Then when you have a few minutes . . .'

As soon as they were alone he began – not with Veeranna but with the little Nataraja. 'Hannah, I think you knew the Shiva had been changed.'

'Of course I know. Miss Sanni say I not to let the houseboys touch it ever. The shelf, yes. I tell them clean carefully, take away flowers and food, but it is I, no other servant, who lift Nataraja to dust it. That how I know, soon as I lift. It not as much heavy.'

'Did you tell Miss Sanni?'

'Indeed I tell and I say to her, "Professor Miss Sahib always telling it very valuable. What should we do, Miss Sanni? Call police?" And I say to her, "What shall I do?"'

'And?'

'"Dust it," she say.'

'And what did you do?'

'As Miss Sanni say,' said Hannah, as if that was the only thing anyone could do.

'Did you tell Samuel?'

'Of course, and Samuel say to me, "You hush."'

——

Michael went in search of the old butler. 'Samuel, where is Chief Inspector Dutta?'

'He gone away, Sahib.'

'I know, but where?'

'I not know, Sahib. He say back tomorrow night,'

and Samuel went on, 'Sahib, I think you take Moses and go to see Veeranna.'

'Yes, I did.'

'Will you tell Samuel why?'

'Because I knew Veeranna had made the new Shiva.'

'Who told you, Sahib?'

'I guessed when I went yesterday to see Veeranna with Inspector Dutta. Veeranna's face told me and this morning he told me in words.'

The bushy eyebrows under the white turban bristled. 'I think you very clever, Sahib, far more clever than police.' Samuel looked at Michael with distrust. And fear, wondered Michael.

He tried to conciliate. 'Samuel, you know I came to help Miss Sanni.'

'Then go away.'

'Samuel!'

'Yes. We all liking you very much, Dean Sahib, but, please, go back England. Do what Miss Sanni say, "Let things be."'

'It's too late. This taking of the real Shiva has become even more serious since your government called in the police – and remember there is Mr Cromartie. Do you want him to have your Shiva?' Samuel shuddered. 'I am afraid, Samuel, that my knowing that Veeranna made the Nataraja is only a first step. I am bound to find out how and why, if I can.'

'But you are on wrong side, Sahib.'

'The wrong side?'

'Yes. I tell you, we know, I Samuel, Hannah, Thambi, but we not say anything ever, not for a thousand thousand rupees, and never to Inspector Dutta. Never. Never.'

━ ～

There was another telephone call for Michael. 'Inspector Dutta,' Kanu told him, as he handed him the receiver.

'Kanu, please go away, right away.' Michael was sure he would try to stay in earshot.

The Inspector began, 'I was sorry to leave you without warning but I had to leave early. I had a hunch, a feeling that I must go by myself, check about the sculptor, Sri Satya Narayana.'

'I knew you weren't satisfied.'

'No, it sounded somehow too convenient.' The Inspector's voice was excited. 'But it was all exactly as Miss Artemis had said. The Master, as they call him here, had died two years ago but his widow is still living in the studio house – it was easy to locate as he was famous. Mrs Narayana did not know anything about the Shiva. He had so many statues here but she was quite certain he could not have done any work on it. She did not seem to remember Miss Artemis taking it away. "But she very well may have," she told me. "She knew us and knew I was still in mourning and she may have thought it best to have come and gone without troubling me. A charming person."

'I asked her,' the Inspector went on, 'if her husband had lately had any unusual contacts with the outside world, and she said there had been some strange things neither he nor she could explain. A few years ago a letter had come. A printed letter, which she showed me with pride, and certainly it was uncommon, being from what seemed to be a world-wide centre of art, the Presidential Central College of Art, Ancient and Modern, with headquarters in New Delhi but offices in London, Paris, New York and Tokyo, their addresses given as post-office box numbers. The letter was most respectful, asking if Sri Satya Narayana, as master sculptor, would take one of their outstanding male students and teach him the original, centuries-old method of making images of the gods in metal, bronze, silver and gold, first carving them in wax. Sri Narayana had not taken apprentices for years but such a truly magnificent fee was offered "that I'm afraid," the widow said almost regretfully, "it made him accept", so he wrote agreeing. There was no reply but suddenly the money arrived. To her amazement it was in cash, quite a bundle, without even a registration or request for a receipt, and with it the pupil. The young man said he was from Bengal, giving his name as Gopal but, she told me, "He was no Bengali, nor did he want to be an apprentice, saying he had his own work to attend to, but for two years he came for six weeks at a time. He seemed to know nothing of the arts centre but someone supplied him with tools. He never told us who. He had great reverence for my husband, who said he was the best pupil he had ever had. He came for two years, then vanished."

'Michael,' the Inspector went on, 'I tried to contact this arts centre in New Delhi. It seemed not to exist. I tried also London, New York, Tokyo, through the police. This is why I have been so long. Yet there is the letter, the money and, above all, the young man. Michael, I believe I am on to something at last.'

'And so am I,' Michael began, but the Inspector was too engrossed in his own story.

'Tomorrow I am going through the statuary with Mrs Narayana to see if there is anything resembling the Shiva.'

'Hem, wait. I must tell you.'

'I'll be back tomorrow. You can tell me then.'

'Hem!' But Inspector Dutta had rung off.

⁓

'Michael,' said Sir John after dinner, 'I have a mind to drop in on Artemis's lecture. I always enjoy listening to her putting it across. She really is very good because she knows her subject so well, yet has a light touch. Come and see.'

101

Considering the long day at Konak, a surprising number of the group were there, and all the young people.

'Konak!' Duke had said, when they came in. 'I'd expected those statues to move me, which was why I went, but they were . . . tremendous. I'm still speechless, and tonight Artemis is going to tell us more about the gods, and how these wonders were made.'

—⁓—

Artemis was in mid-speech, standing before a table on which was a small collection of images, small because, like all experienced lecturers, she never said too much. These, Michael knew, were the household *puja*-corner gods, probably borrowed from Veeranna. On a pedestal was the niche's Shiva, and as Sir John and Michael came in, she drew it to the centre, saying, 'I should like to tell you how ten, eleven, twelve centuries ago, this little dancing Shiva was made.'

She was in her uniform, long black silk skirt and frilled blouse, her hair tied with the usual chiffon scarf but tonight it was of a flaunting emerald green. She loves colours, thought Michael, and knows how they fit an occasion.

On the table various tools and photographs were laid; her voice was as clear and natural as a bell. 'The master sculptors of that time were not primitive as, for instance, early African art is primitive. In its very

102

simplicity, their art has a remarkable sophistication, as has that of the Greeks. They put us to shame with our modern sculptors and their technical appliances from such amenable things as plastic-covered wire with which they can make a structure, the brilliant lights on stands which can be heightened or lowered and moved. These old masters worked by daylight on the floor of, probably, an open-fronted hut – no trace of a studio – or at night with a small oil lamp. This particular method is called *cire perdu*, or "lost wax", but thank God, there are still a few artists left who can do it.

'To begin with the god is carved in wax, hard, yellowish in colour, the texts say, beautiful to behold, because it is now that the master shows his greatest skill as each line, each expression will eventually be reproduced exactly, and it has to be in proportion with the things the god carries, such as a sword, a drum or *vina*, maybe a reptile, all attributes given by the ancient scripts. The carving takes a long time. When it's finished it's given a light coating of clay, carefully mixed with charred husks, tiny bits of cotton and salt, all ground by hand on a stone until they are powder. Then the god is left to dry in the shade. This coating of clay is done three times, at intervals of two days, and each time it is heavier.

'Long tubes with a flared mouth resembling the *kusa* flower are added through the wax on the back, the shoulders, on the nape of the neck and crown of the head and have to be kept open, not blocked by the clay.

'The weight of the finished image has been decided by the weight of the finished wax figure, eight times heavier for bronze, twelve for silver, sixteen for gold. This Shiva is bronze. On the chosen day when the clay mould is hard enough, it is put in an earthenware crucible to withstand great heat and set in a fire. The wax melts and runs out. Meanwhile the metal has been heated until it is liquid. Then, holding its container with a pair of tongs, the artist pours the liquid quickly into the mouths of the tubes until they are filled to the brim. The figure now has to cool. Then the master breaks off the clay mould bit by bit. When the whole is revealed he will know if he has succeeded, and if he can cut away the mouths of the tubes making them level and give his god or goddess its finishing touches.

'The text ends,' said Artemis, 'with a royal instruction. On an auspicious day the King should install it where it can be worshipped every day with offerings, flowers and a light, which our Shiva is,' said Artemis.

'But, Artemis,' said Eric Barclay, 'isn't that Shiva the one which was stolen? The trial is coming up in London. It's made such a sensation.'

'Yes.'

'Then what *is* this one?'

How, wondered Michael, with her deep regard

for Auntie Sanni and her own wishes, would Artemis field that?

'This is the one that was not stolen,' she said, and went on too quickly for Eric to say anything more. 'You have listened so politely to me that we'll change the subject and Ellen will show you a film I had made last year of the Ghandara hills' cave paintings.'

'Professor Ellen has a headache,' Sir John whispered to her.

'All the same, she'll have to do it. I've had enough,' Artemis whispered back, and went on, 'We had only a small unit, the cameraman and one soundman, but it came out quite well. You'll see. We're going to the caves tomorrow.'

When the film ended and the audience came out, it was plain they were not only interested but exuberant. There were congratulations, tumultuous questions, drinks, talk, laughter.

'I've already learned so much I can't take it all in,' confessed Duke. 'I'll have to come back.'

'I've learned so much I shall never forget,' said Madame Duvivier. But Michael was in no humour for any of it. His mind was seething with problems as he went further up the veranda, past Auntie Sanni, and leaned on the rail hoping to become part of the calm of the garden until he felt someone beside him. Artemis. She was so close they were almost touching, but as he turned to her, she drew away. She was angry.

'Michael,' she said, 'when we came back I didn't want to rest. Konak always has that effect on me, it's too exciting, so I went into the village to see some of my friends. I have been coming here for a long time. Patna Hall and the village have been very useful to me – they are why I learned Telegu. Of course I went to Veeranna – he's a very special friend – but as soon as he saw me he burst into tears. He says you tricked him into telling you he made the new Shiva.'

'I didn't trick him. When I saw him with Inspector Dutta I guessed. This morning I asked him outright and he admitted it – with delight, Artemis.'

'Then he was lying.'

'I don't think Veeranna lies.'

But Artemis argued, 'How could he have made it? He hasn't any tools. You didn't use your senses, Michael.'

'You're right. I'm supposed to be a barrister and at this stage barristers are never allowed to cross-examine witnesses – that's a solicitor's job, and here I am behaving like a solicitor. What's come over me? It's as if I'm under a spell. You all tell me that Veeranna couldn't have made the Shiva, but I know he did. I know, too, he won't tell me how or why.'

'No. He won't ever.'

'But I have a nasty feeling that Chief Inspector Dutta and his crew have ways of making him.'

She looked at him in horror. 'Must you tell Inspector Dutta?'

'Artemis, I have a professional duty.'

'Prig.'

'That's not fair.'

She came closer. 'Michael, please don't tell the police – for Veeranna's sake. He's such an innocent, and didn't dream he was doing anything wrong. Just for once, Michael,' and she gave him a kiss, light as a butterfly's wing on his cheek. 'Promise.'

'I can't,' said Michael. 'I must tell the Inspector as soon as I see him.'

'Then I hate you,' flashed Artemis, and left him.

———

The group had to leave Patna Hall at seven to get to the caves.

'We'll get up at five and walk,' said Duke.

'If I were you I don't think I would,' said Artemis. 'It's sixteen miles. The coach will take us as far as it can, which is twelve miles, then there are four miles of steep rough walking. There will be ponies for those who would rather ride.'

'Perhaps it would be better if I don't come,' said one of the older members. 'After all, we saw the beautiful film last night – but I hope you don't think I'm a coward.'

'I wouldn't think of coming.' That was Mrs Moaner who, for some reason, had got up. 'Not after yesterday. I don't want to see any more of this horrible Indian art. Filthy. Sex crazy. I felt sick, and they call them gods. I was too ashamed to look at them.'

'Then you didn't see them,' said Madame Duvivier.

'The cave paintings are of animals, not humans,' Artemis interposed quickly.

'Animals might be worse. Oh dear.' Mrs Moaner was ready to weep. 'We never seem to do anything nice.'

'Wait for tonight,' said Artemis. 'Professor Ellen will make an announcement at lunch. There's an invitation I think you will like.' She could have added, 'I hope,' but not very hopefully, and returned to the cave paintings. 'Those ancient masters were marvellously gifted. They could draw and paint so that the creatures seem to breathe and live.'

'On rough walls?' Mrs Moaner sniffed in derision.

'That is the wonder, and they had no choice. Remember, there were no canvases then, no paper, indeed no houses. Besides, the paintings were of the utmost importance. To those cave dwellers, animals were far more important than humans because they lived by their hunting, and the people in their innocence believed that if they could catch the likeness on their walls of those birds, wild oxen, bison, wolves, even tigers, they would catch them in reality.'

'Judging by the film, they have been caught,' said Madame Duvivier.

Marcia Barclay enthused, 'Artemis, you make everything so interesting. Will you go through it again?'

'I think Professor Ellen will. I have to go and see a little temple I've heard of higher in the hills.'

'I wish she wouldn't,' Professor Ellen said to Michael, who had got up early to see them off – and also because this was the time when the gardeners came in to decorate the shrine. 'Michael, it isn't safe for a girl to go alone into the hills. I wish you'd speak to her. She might listen to you.'

'Artemis and I are not very good friends just now but I'll try.'

He managed to catch her just as she was leaving for the coach. 'I hear that when you get to the caves you're going off on your own.'

'What business is it of yours?' She was still hostile.

'It's the business of anyone who cares about you.'

She looked up into his face. 'Michael, I think you do care.'

'Haven't I shown it from the first moment?'

She relented. 'Well, don't worry. I don't go alone. I go with a friend and his servant.'

After breakfast Michael went to find Auntie Sanni, who was in her office. 'May I have your permission to ask all your staff a few questions?'

'Inspector Dutta did that the day before yesterday without asking.'

'Inspector Dutta and I have different ways. I'd like to see them one by one, but it will have to be through Moses. May I?'

'Do you really need to?'

'I mustn't leave any stone unturned.'

'These are people not stones.'

'I'll be very gentle, Auntie Sanni.'

***

Michael saw the gardeners first and had Moses ask each one the same question. 'You come every morning to bring fresh flowers for the god. Are you sure you never noticed that he was not the same?'

The answers varied.

'No.'

'He always there. How could we think he not the same?'

'I not look at him very much.'

'I busy with the flowers.'

But they all added up to 'No.'

The Muslim table waiters, Abdul and Karim, both wearing off-duty clothes, were unhelpful, even scornful.

'He Hindu god,' said Karim. 'I never look.'

'I not want to look,' said Abdul.

The Nepali houseboys, Kancha and Jetta, seemed always on duty, yet cheerful, but they said, 'Shiva statue. We not even dust it. Hannah not allow us. How can we know?'

Colonel McIndoe's valet, a servant with a position below Samuel and Hannah's but above the other servants, was contemptuous. 'It great fuss. How can Hindu god be so important? As for me, I never go into drawing room unless there is reception or ceremony when I go in charge of drinks and I far, far too busy to look.'

The sweeper women were more observant, chanting hymns to him as they bumped along the floor with their bottles – but they were too many to interrogate separately. 'Of course he our Shiva, always is, always same,' they all agreed.

'That's a morning wasted,' said Michael, downcast.

'Try Kanu,' said Hannah. 'He say anything for money.'

Michael thought she was mocking him.

⸻

He did not have to go to Kanu. Kanu came to him. 'Sahib Michael. How much will you give me if I tell you what I tell Mr Cromartie in London?'

'Nothing,' said Michael. 'I happen to know what you told Mr Cromartie.'

Kanu's mouth fell open in dismay and puzzlement. 'How you know?'

'My business,' said Michael, 'but I'll buy you a

drink if you'll tell me that what you told him in London is true. Don't forget, I'm investigating. Gin and tonic?'

'Samuel, he skin me.'

'Not if I give it to you.'

'You so nice, Michael, but you not know Samuel. He not let me drink one glass. I not stay here. Michael, I going to be barman at Uberoi hotel, Mr Cromartie he say so. He pay me very well. You know why?' Kanu came closer. 'Not only information, I think, but because I am so very pretty.'

Pretty? thought Michael. Yes, if you like that sort of thing.

'Long, long ago when I was small boy I got into trouble here – trouble that for me fine but Hannah make it bad and ever since,' he took a gulp of gin, 'no one trust me. Ten o'clock, I must go home – my people live in the village. If I late my father come to fetch me. But, Michael, I not little boy now. I grown up, Michael, for little money if you want?'

'Kanu, I am not Mr Cromartie.'

Kanu grew spiteful. 'You wrong. I not only pretty. Kanu know who took the Shiva and why.'

'You know why?'

'Yes. Kanu put two and two together.' He was getting excited. 'The Colonel, Auntie Sanni, they get old. My father and mother think Samuel and Hannah like gods, everything good, but Hannah, she there when Professor Ellen took first Shiva figure down for lecture and Hannah she hear what Professor tell Auntie Sanni how much it was valuable – millions of rupees,' said Kanu, his eyes wide. 'Hannah, she tell Samuel.'

'So you think . . .?'

Kanu put his finger one side of his nose and winked in glee. 'Aha! Now you listen. Auntie Sanni, she old, soon die. Without Auntie Sanni, Patna Hall die too, or else so few people coming, Patna Hall close. What Samuel and Hannah do then? They also old, too old to get other job. What they do then?'

'I'm sure the Colonel would look after them.'

'Maybe, maybe not, and maybe Samuel and Hannah want – how do you say? Nest . . .?'

'Nest egg.' Michael put down his glass. 'Where you going?'

'To ask them.'

'*Ask!*' Kanu was startled. 'I think better you tell Police Inspector Dutta.'

'I don't think Inspector Dutta will be interested.'

'Then you don't believe me.'

'I believe you are a nasty little liar,' but Kanu did not know the meaning of the word nasty.

— ⌣ —

Michael found Samuel in the pantry behind the dining room having a tumbler of tea before starting to get ready for luncheon. He was in a loose shirt, his impressive turban laid aside, but as soon as he saw

Michael he stood up, set down the tumbler and put it on.

'Samuel, have your tea. I only want a few words with you.' Michael sat on a stool.

Reluctantly Samuel sat too. 'Tea for you, Sahib?'

'No, thank you. I had a drink with Kanu. If that was wrong it's my fault, not his.'

'Not easy boy. Hannah and I, we fear for him. His father and mother most nice people.'

'Miss Sanni will help him. Samuel, may I talk to you a little about Patna Hall?'

Samuel was relieved. 'Ah, the hotel. If I can help you . . .'

'You can if you will. I know it had a great heyday.'

'Heyday, Sahib?'

'A time of great success. What has changed it?'

'Patna Hall not changed, not one i-o-ta.' Samuel was proud he knew that word. 'Not us. It is visitors. They want quick, quick, quick, airflight everywhere, they not stay. Business people, schedule. Tourist hurry, get so many things in one package. Patna Hall not like that at all so not many people come.' Samuel spread his hands helplessly. 'And we getting old, Sahib.'

'Yes,' and Michael said gently, 'Miss Sanni and Colonel McIndoe too.' Then, he quoted Kanu. 'If they close Patna Hall, I think you and Hannah are too old to get other work.'

'Other work? Never, never. They look after us.'

'If the hotel is losing money, they may be too poor.'

'If they poor, we poor. We be proud to share. Hannah, me and Thambi.'

Michael could only say, 'I beg your pardon, Samuel.'

'Sahib ask pardon of me!' The old man was plainly gratified. 'Sahib—' He stopped as if some thought had suddenly struck him. 'Michael Sahib, you London lawyer, very clever. The Nataraja, is it of so great value as they say?'

'The experts think so. They valued it at more than two hundred and fifty thousand pounds.'

'Ah!' Samuel shuddered, and Michael seized what he was sure was an opportunity.

'May I ask you a question myself? You needn't answer if you don't want to.'

'Ask, Sahib,' but Samuel was bowed down in distress.

'You seem so unhappy and worried,' and Michael dared to go on, 'Is it because you and Hannah believe that what Kanu says is true?'

There was a silence. Then, 'Yes,' said Samuel, and he seemed to brace himself and stood up. 'All these days Hannah and I, Thambi too, not tell you because we so frightened for Miss Sanni. Yes, we not saying anything, anything at all. We so much afraid. The one who took the Shiva for to sell it was Miss Sanni. Of course, Colonel Sahib help her. Michael

115

Sahib, she only do it to save Patna Hall, but now . . . oh, what happen to Miss Sanni? Now there is Inspector Dutta, London lawyers, our government. What happen to her?'

'It couldn't have been Miss Sanni.'

'Couldn't? I tell you, Sahib . . .'

'I know, but you are wrong.'

'How?'

'For the best of reasons. Because she is Miss Sanni. She would never have sold the Shiva, not even for Patna Hall. Miss Sanni believes in reverence for everyone else's gods, and her own – that before anything else.'

'Then who?' said Samuel uncertainly.

'We don't know, but not Miss Sanni.'

Light broke on Samuel's face. He got up and rushed through the dining room. 'Hannah! Hannah!'

She came quickly. 'Michael Sahib know,' Samuel told her. 'He so much more clever than us. He say Miss Sanni she never never sell the Shiva.' And he repeated what Michael had said.

As she listened the same light came on Hannah's face, tears too. 'Samuel, Michael Sahib right. He completely right. Me, I know it now. I know it in my bones, but we in so much fright. Not thinking properly. God bless you, Michael Sahib. God bless you.'

116

Michael felt he must try to clear his head so he went down to the beach for a swim – and did not swim.

Back from the caves, some of the young were there too, ready to go into the sea when Moses and his fishermen could take them. Thambi was up on the diving board with Artemis.

Although most of the day had been wasted, Michael, now susceptible, had this unaccustomed happiness in his heart and he stood to watch her, her body wet and ready poised, until there came another spectacular dive far over the others in the water who clapped. But Michael did not want to be drawn into chat just now, not even with Artemis, and he went back to the house.

Auntie Sanni was on her swing couch as he came up the steps to the veranda and he felt he must thank her for letting him interview the servants.

'Well, did you find out anything?'

'Not a thing towards a solution but I didn't expect to.'

Auntie Sanni laid her hand on his arm and said what Samuel had said: 'Michael, we have all come to like you – honour you, too – but please, Michael, give this up and go back to London.'

'It's what I came for.'

'Still, go back. Michael, I see nothing but pain, sorrow and hurt.'

'Auntie Sanni, if justice is done someone has to be hurt.'

'That will be terrible.'

'Not for me. I can't go now.' And, with a sudden rush of the confidence that people felt with Auntie Sanni and a flood of happiness, 'Because this work is not all. Through you and Patna Hall, I know something now that has never touched me before.'

'Artemis,' said Auntie Sanni.

Michael got up. He still did not want to talk about it, but as he went down the veranda he thought he heard Auntie Sanni say, 'Oh dear! Oh dear! Oh dear!'

———

At the end of lunch Professor Ellen stood up and waited until a hush fell on the cleared table. 'This evening we come to what I hope you will find the highlight of our tour. Our brochure simply lists "evening visit to the old town of Konakpur and its palace, the Gul Mahal", which gives little inkling of what that means. The old town is fascinating. It has a whole street of carved house fronts, an inland lake and overlooking it, high on a steep hill, the Maharajah's palace, the Gul Mahal, which means Rose Palace in honour of the thousands of roses on its terraces. Of course, the Maharajah is not a Maharajah now. He lives on the French Riviera, but the Government let him keep the palace on condition that he opened it to the public. But we do not go as the public. By his special command, his steward invites us every year to a banquet. First you will see the State apartments. They include a famous room where the furniture is made of glass.'

'Glass!' Marcia interrupted.

'Yes, chairs and tables, and there is jewellery. Then the banquet, and afterwards a display of dancing in the pavilion built on the roof. The way up to the palace is by three paths, the chief being the central one which has stone steps with ramps where fountains used to play. On one side is the elephant path. There is a high archway at the top to let them go in but, sadly, there is only one elephant now.'

'Oh dear! I'll never get up,' moaned Mrs Moaner.

'You will, because on the other side there is a smooth path between the ramps. It was for the court ladies' light rickshaws, which needed two men each, one to pull, the other to push behind. The rickshaws are still there – they are inlaid with mother-of-pearl.'

'I've never ridden in a rickshaw.' Mrs Moaner was beginning to sound mollified.

'The banquet will have Indian and European food, drinks and wine, and afterwards we go up to the pavilion for coffee. It really is an enchantment – so high it seems to be in the sky, to which it is open. Its walls are ivory, carved and latticed, its floor has marble squares with silk-covered couches along the walls for the watchers of the entertainments given there almost every night.

'We shall see a display of classical Indian dancing,

the famous Bharata Natyam on which the Maharajah doted. Before it begins, Artemis will explain it to you, as she does so well. I know you have had a long morning, but I hope you will all come. It really shouldn't be missed, so please be ready at five. Thank you.'

After lunch, when they were having coffee on the veranda, Artemis came up to Michael and, linking arms with him, drew him apart. 'Michael, why don't you come?'

'I thought you hated me.'

'That was what my mother used to call "temporary temper". Please come.'

'I shouldn't – I've got work to do – but it sounds so tempting.'

'Then be tempted. Auntie Sanni says Inspector Dutta is not coming back until late. I purposely asked her and there is nothing you can do until he comes. Samuel says you have been working hard all morning. Besides . . . Oh, Michael, I have been back and forth on the coach listening to the chatter, never getting away from the questions, and I have to give quite an important talk tonight. I really do need time to think. Wouldn't you drive me? If you will, we needn't go to the city. Shall we say four o'clock? And you can see the Gul Mahal before the others come. It really is magical.'

'I think I'm ready for a little magic,' said Michael.

The way led first along the seashore then left the feathery trees and dunes for the hard sand and palms that ended in a road through the foothills, planted with what Michael thought was coffee. Soon the hills grew steep.

'Have you ever been to Konakpur?' asked Artemis.

'Nowhere near this coast. We were in Peshawar at Pindi.'

Artemis was wearing a short sleeveless dress, brilliant orange – for this occasion she was out of her uniform – but her hair was still up in a knob with a matching chiffon scarf; its ends fluttered in the breeze from the car window. Michael was in rhythm with it and he began to sing: '*Take a pair of sparkling eyes, / hidden ever and anon, in a beautiful eclipse . . .*' The light rollicking tune filled the car.

'Oh, Michael, I do so like being with you.'

'And I love being with you.'

He stopped the car, turned, put his arm round her and kissed her. This time she did not pull away but returned the kiss. Her lips were warm and he found her tongue between the pretty little teeth until, 'Michael, we must get on.'

As they drove, Artemis said, 'To me Konakpur is the most beautiful of any Indian city I know. They call it the Rose City. You'll see why.'

Now they began to pass hamlets and villages where there were only a few stone houses or modern bungalows; small bazaars, almost empty now – the people were still in the fields – then, rounding a corner, looked down on the town. Set in a valley with a lake, it still had its walls, built of the pinkish local stone. 'Seventeenth century,' said Artemis. 'One of the great maharajahs built it, laying it out like a map, which is why its streets and boulevards are so wide, with the narrow streets of carved house fronts between. He must have been fabulously rich, and had a great eye for beauty. At sunset I have seen the stone turn to rose, especially the Gul Mahal.'

They stopped at a wide platform at the foot of the three steep flights of steps, built of darker, almost red, blocks of stone; the parallel elephant and rickshaw paths were smooth to the palace walls high above, crowned with what Michael guessed was the pavilion Professor Ellen had described.

He stood gazing until Artemis said, 'I want you to meet a friend of mine. It's partly why I brought you.' Turning, she made a call towards a building like a barn beside the platform, a call that sounded as if it were blown through a conch: ulla, ullalah, ullahh. There were immediate commands and the sound of a soft heavy tread, tread, tread, until an elephant appeared. Even for an elephant he was a giant, his grey wrinkled skin glinting in the late-afternoon sun, the big tusks banded with gold, the huge ears gently flapping so that the spotted undersides showed as his great feet moved steadily forward. Michael had forgotten how large an elephant's toenails were. Don't elephants' eyes see multiple aspects? thought Michael. These eyes, surprisingly small, black and bright, were looking expectant.

The elephant had a howdah on his back, with red padded seats and curtains, rather frayed, and on his neck sat a wizened little man who, as they neared Artemis, prodded the great forehead with his *ankus*. 'Salaam,' but the elephant had already salaamed, raising his trunk to his forehead three times in joy.

'This is Natram, the friend I told you about. Natram means precious jewel,' said Artemis, 'and Mahdhoo is his mahout and servant, though Mahdhoo drives him and Natram obeys. Mahdhoo looks after him, day and night,' and she said to the elephant, who was shifting his feet, 'Just have patience,' as she patted his trunk. Then she went back to the car, opened the boot and took out a whole stem of bananas. She stood breaking them off, three at a time, peeling them, then putting them into the pink-nozzled trunk, held out before Natram stuffed them into his mouth, pink too. When the last of the bananas had disappeared, she said, 'You see why I feel utterly safe with them when I go into the hills. I only have to send a message and Mahdhoo meets me.'

'*Khachitamuya*,' said Mahdhoo. 'Yes, indeed.'

'Will they take us up?' asked Michael. 'It's years since I've ridden on an elephant.'

'Of course. That's why I called them. If I hadn't, neither of them would forgive me. Come. He'll kneel and we'll get up on to the howdah.' Then Artemis stopped, her hand clapped to her mouth in dismay. 'Michael,' she wailed, 'I've forgotten my notes.'

'Notes?'

'I told you, I've got to give a talk tonight.'

'Couldn't you improvise?'

'You don't understand. It's on Bharata Natyam, which is perhaps the highest of India's four classical dance styles, terribly difficult to explain to an audience whose idea of Indian dancing is the *nautch* girl, almost akin to a belly dancer and who can usually be had for money. A Bharata Natyam dancer is the echo of the *asparas*, or celestial dancers of heaven, who dance for the gods. You'll see. Before each begins she makes a deep obeisance to the god, and never turns her back on him. More than that, every least movement has a meaning – the hand movements, for instance, have names like Lotus Bud, Deer's Head, Swan's Neck.'

'Who is to know if you make a mistake?'

'The dancers would know and it would be blasphemy. They would never dance for us again. They have been through years and years of strict training and most of them speak English. I must have the notes. If you would lend me your car I'll whiz back and fetch them and still be in plenty of time.

124

You go up on Natram and explore. I don't want you to miss the banquet.'

'I'm coming with you,' said Michael.

⸻

As they drew up under Patna Hall's portico, Artemis had the car door open and was out. 'I'll try not to be too long but I must make sure I have everything. Perhaps twenty minutes.'

'I'll wait,' said Michael.

It was peaceful under the portico. Patna Hall seemed silent. I expect they're changing for dinner, he thought. The servants will be having theirs and Kanu is at the bar. The hall was empty. Thambi's lodge was lit inside but he himself had gone with the party, chiefly to help pull the rickshaws up the hill. In the village beyond the palm trees, where points of lantern light had appeared, smoke was going up from cooking fires for the evening meal. Outside, dust was rising from the paths as the last of the cattle were driven home. 'Cow-dust time', he remembered from his boyhood.

He was peaceful and filled with a happiness that no one, not Auntie Sanni, not even himself, could gainsay, and he began quietly to hum.

'I know where I am going,' but instead of 'Dear knows who I'll marry', he hummed, 'I know where I'm going and I do know who I'll marry. I've found her.' But the minutes were ticking away. Twenty? More like forty.

When Artemis appeared she seemed out of breath. 'I'm sorry, but there were bits I had to reread. Oh, Michael, you're so patient – and hungry too by now, I'm sure. I hope you don't miss the banquet.'

'I'll drive like the wind.'

Artemis settled herself and said, 'In Hindi, to go fast in a car is called *howa khana*, which means "to eat the air". You eat the air but I think I'll go to sleep.'

She lay back and closed her eyes but he knew she was not asleep. Is she fending me off? he thought, in a moment's anxiety, but as if in answer, she smiled and patted his knee.

When he pulled up on the platform, Natram and Mahdhoo were waiting, ready to take them up.

Although he was voraciously hungry, Michael tasted little of the banquet. Innumerable dishes were offered to him: small balls of lamb in an apricot coating, koftas, tandoori chicken, fish, every sort of rice, there was even a side of beef, all on platters that were silver, though they were more than a little stained. There were knives and forks but some of the young or more enthusiastic, like Marcia Barclay, ate with their fingers – to Eric's disgust. After the main course, shallow silver bowls filled with rose water were passed for the guests to wash their fingers. Then came heaped stands of Indian sweets: the edible silver paper on the *sandesh* toffee glittered, and there were *jilipis*, rings of spun sugar dripping with honey, and sliced fresh fruit. Wine was served, and sherbet,

126

orange juice, whisky, yet Mrs Moaner was heard saying loudly, 'It's all very well but the Indians have no standards – tarnished silver, chipped plates.' Michael, who prided himself on assessing everything with a cool head, ate and drank as if he were in a dream.

Afterwards when everyone had finished, they trooped up a marble staircase, led by Professor Ellen, for coffee and liqueurs in the pavilion, which was lit only by torches. A wide space was left in the centre but all round were divans and daybeds on which the guests could recline as they watched. 'It's not always like this,' Professor Ellen told them. She was astute enough to make the point for her tours. 'This is only for us. I think you must agree we are privileged.'

There was a chorus of 'Yes.'

The musicians were already seated on a carpet, all dressed alike in white silk tunics and flowing *dhotis*: a *tabla* drum player with two drums, a flautist with a silver flute, two sitars and, as a concession to a Western audience, a violin.

When everyone was seated, coffee and liqueurs over, Artemis stood up, and the excited chatter fell to a murmur as a single dancer came in, an older woman, beautiful in her brilliant gauze silks, her sari looped up into a pleated fan from her waist to her ankles on which she wore circlets of golden bells that tinkled as she moved. The short bodice was of silk showing her midriff bare. She had many necklaces, ear-rings and flowers bunched close in her hair, with a pendant on her forehead above her *tika* mark of red henna. She wore only one bangle, however, on each upper arm, because her hands had to be free; they were so supple that they seemed almost to double straight backwards and forwards as she illustrated in movement everything Artemis described, beginning with the deep obeisance to her god. She did not smile but spoke with her eyes.

As Michael knew already, Artemis had a way of making the most technical lecture into a talk that was vividly alive but tonight she seemed incandescent, perhaps catching it from the dancers. And I have found her, Michael marvelled in his deepest heart.

As the first dancer reached her finale the others came in, taking up their positions; the musicians went straight into the long elaborately exquisite dance. When it ended, the dancers repeating their obeisance, the applause was deafening. Everyone seemed lit with enthusiasm. This night will never die, thought Michael.

It was not over yet. When the dancing was finished, and the applause had petered out, cold drinks were served and, for those who wanted it, whisky. The dancers had disappeared. Professor Ellen announced that the coach was ready. Several ladies took advantage of the rickshaws – 'I wish I could,' said Eric Barclay, as he stumbled down the steep steps. Mrs Moaner had fallen asleep, and was carried down tenderly in a rickshaw by Thambi and the palace servants. Last to go was Professor Ellen.

'I'll follow you with Michael,' said Artemis.

They stayed in the pavilion where the torches had been doused so that the court was lit only by starlight. Although corners were dark, the marble floor glimmered and the ivory lattices were slanted with light. 'Why do stars seem bigger in India than at home?' asked Artemis, and put her arms round his neck. She moved her cheek against his; it was as hot as if she had a fever. She left him, went to a corner and drew back a heavy silk curtain to show a canopied room with a wide divan, covered in brocade. 'This is where the Maharajah used to end his entertainments, picking anyone he fancied that night. Do you fancy me, Michael?'

For answer Michael caught and held her, and carried her to the divan.

'Come, my Maharajah.'

⚊ ⚊

It was like fire, rockets. 'Oh, Michael. Again.'

⚊ ⚊

They were late reaching home. The watchman of the Gul Mahal, plainly accustomed to this, had left them as long as he could. Then, 'Sahib, Memsahib' – Artemis had been elevated to Mem – 'we must lock

up or police come. Very sorry but must.' As he had
hoped, Michael gave him a mighty tip.

Natram and Mahdhoo had not waited but
Michael and Artemis made their way down, she
dancing on every ramp, Michael catching her to kiss
her again. The starlight gave them just enough light
to see. 'I expect everyone else will be asleep,' Artemis
said in the car, as they came near to Patna Hall.

'Well, we don't want anyone else,' said Michael.
Then, 'Hush! What's this?'

Thambi's lodge, the hall and portico, the servants'
quarters were lit, as was the village where a crowd of
people was standing. A drum was beating a long,
steady sound. 'Something's happened.' As Michael
pulled up under the portico, opened the door and
got out, Samuel, who evidently had waited up, came
to meet them. His face was grave. 'Sahib, thank God
you come. Missy Sahib, be brave. Veeranna, he dead.'

—◦—

'Veeranna!' Artemis's cry rang through the hall. She
had gone white.

'But how?' Michael, stunned, could hardly speak.

'Evening time. A woman passing heard scream,
noises, a commotion, and ran to fetch her husband.
Veeranna on floor, twisting, doubling up and retch,
retch, retch. Husband try to hold him but Veeranna
too strong. Woman run for village barber.'

'Barber?'

130

'In villages no doctors so barbers are only medicine men. He try everything. No use. Veeranna, he die. Barber say poison.'

'Poison!' Artemis screamed. 'Michael, hold me! Hold me tight.' Michael was already holding her, trying to stop the shaking, stem the screams between the dry sobs, no tears, but Hannah came down the stairs.

'Now, now,' said Hannah. 'That enough.' She took Artemis from Michael, who stood helpless. 'It shock, Sahib,' Hannah told him, 'and maybe too much exciting today. You tired out, *baba*. Hannah put you to bed. I just put Miss Sanni to bed,' she told Michael over Artemis's head. 'Now, *baba*, come with Hannah.'

To Michael's surprise, Artemis went.

Samuel looked after them. 'Missy Sahib, she friend of all the village, most of all Veeranna. I think all of us in shock, Michael Sahib.'

'Yes. What did they do when he died?'

'They send for Miss Sanni – always they send for Miss Sanni – but it was Colonel McIndoe Sahib who came. He turn everyone out of the workshop and made them keep distance. He find Inspector Dutta by telephone, who say he come quickly as he can. Meanwhile no one must go in or touch anything. Colonel put Thambi – he just back on the coach – in front, village headman behind, young policeman to patrol. People must go back to their homes.'

'If they will,' said Michael.

'I think they watch,' Samuel agreed. Michael

turned away from the portico steps. 'Sahib, they let no one in.'

'I won't go near. I only want to see what is happening now.'

As he came close the drumbeat sounded louder, and he was right: the crowd of men was still standing under the trees; women were wailing in their houses. When he saw Michael, Thambi, who had been sitting on his haunches, stood up. 'It's all right, Thambi, I know I mustn't go in. I just came to see how things were.'

Thambi averted his head so as not to show Michael his grief. 'Sahib very good. Good night.'

'Not a good night now. This is bad,' said Michael. A great weariness was overtaking him as he went back.

'Samuel, is Missy Sahib in bed?' he managed to ask.

'Hannah say, soon as she lie down she asleep, tired out.'

'Me too.' Michael tottered as he spoke. 'I'm sorry to desert you but I think I'll have to go to bed.' He could hardly reach the stairs and had to hold on to the banisters, but Samuel was beside him and steered him to his room.

He fell on his bed and was only just aware of Samuel taking off his shoes and covering him with a blanket before he slept.

'Michael! Michael, wake up.' It was a fierce whisper in his ear, and someone was shaking him firmly. 'Wake up!'

'But I've only just gone to sleep.'

'It's morning.'

He sat up, trying to fight off layers of sleep. 'It's dark.'

He was about to turn over, back into sleep again, when he realized it was Artemis. 'Artemis. What's happening?'

'Ssh!' She pulled off the blanket. 'Thank God you're dressed. Find your shoes and come on. There's something I want to show you.'

'Now? It's still dark.'

'Not outside. It's dawn. Hurry, before anyone is up.'

Still half asleep, he put on his shoes, smoothed his rumpled clothes, ran a comb through his hair.

'Never mind that. We need to go before anyone's awake, and it's quite a way.'

But Michael had recovered his senses. 'I can't be long. I have to see Inspector Dutta as soon as he comes.'

'There's plenty of time to do that. Come on.'

At the foot of the stairs he turned towards the portico but she stopped him. 'Not that way. We'll go along the beach – then the village won't see us.'

'Us?'

'You and me. Natram and Mahdhoo.'

'They're here!'

'I ordered them. You see, I planned this yesterday.'

They went through the garden, still wet with dew – soon the gardeners would be flailing the lawns with long bamboo rods to stop the sun scorching the wet grass – and, as Artemis and Michael came on to the beach, there beside the high diving board, the great shape of Natram stood waiting and ready.

Mahdhoo and Natram salaamed, then the elephant knelt down. There was no howdah, only a pad fastened with ropes. Mahdhoo stretched down to give Artemis a hand but she was so lithe that she swung herself up easily. Michael was more clumsy: he put his foot against Natram's side to lever himself up on a rope, and slipped back. Mahdhoo spoke. Natram turned his head and his trunk came round: Michael felt its enormous strength as he was lifted up so that he could scramble on to the pad. Artemis laughed. 'Sometimes Natram just picks me up and puts me on his back.'

Natram stood up and began to walk along the beach.

It was beginning to be light, with the sky brightening over the sea, the surf in the waves shining white. Natram walked through the ripples, which he seemed to like, spraying his legs as he went. Do elephants get footsore, Michael wondered. He was surprised, too, at how fast Natram went with a half-rolling, half-swaying gait. It almost lulled him to sleep again.

As soon as they were far enough out of the village, Mahdhoo turned Natram inland. They went through a patch of jungle towards the hills. Natram was a well-trained elephant: if a branch overhung their way, at a command from Mahdhoo, his trunk came up to break it off, in case it hit his passengers. When they came out from the trees on to a swampy patch he tested the ground with a cautious foot before he would venture. Presently they began to climb into the cooler air of the hills. Again, Michael would have gone to sleep but he was aware of Artemis, sitting upright. She seemed oddly tense, her face, in the growing dawn light, resolute and stern.

'Artemis?'

'Ssh.'

'But where are you taking me?'

'You'll see – and see why.'

◆～

'It is something that, of us all, only Auntie Sanni and I know.'

Natram had begun to go downwards instead of climbing and there, in a cleft of the hills, inset so that it looked across higher hills to a vista of the sea, was a little temple. As the elephant went steadily down an old path and they came nearer, Michael saw that it was walled with small bricks, perhaps made of natural earth, baked in the sun; in the growing light they were already touched with faint gold. The roof had a dome of tiles that matched, and there was a small portico of stone in which hung a bell. 'No one but I has rung it for years. No one comes here now, not even a priest,' said Artemis.

Natram had knelt to let them get down and Mahdhoo took from the pad a bundle of sugar cane. 'Natram's breakfast,' said Artemis. 'I wish I could have brought tea for us but I didn't want anyone to see us go.'

'*Kachiyundu*, stay,' Mahdhoo told Natram, as he stood up.

'Mahdhoo loves this temple,' said Artemis. 'Come and look.'

The courtyard was small, and had in its centre a statue of a bull carved from local stone. It stood looking into the temple, and its eyes, as if in awe, were strangely eloquent. 'He seems to see something there,' said Michael.

'He does,' and Artemis explained, 'He is Nandi, Shiva's emblem. Hindu gods love their animal representatives, and as Shiva is new life, women pray to Nandi for a son.'

'Would you like a son, Artemis?'

'If it could be with the person I love. Yes.'

He would have taken her in his arms and kissed her but she said, 'No, Michael, not here,' and she told him, 'Auntie Sanni, when she was younger, used to come here to make her *puja* and so do I.'

'To Shiva?'

'Shiva and God.'

Artemis swung the tasselled bell, sending its deep note far over the hills. 'Go in, Michael.'

The temple was almost bare: there was only a low shelf with a tray holding *dipas* – little lamps of clay shaped like a leaf – but there was no oil in them, no tiny floating wick. On the floor was a small fireplace made of bricks and full of cold ash; by it a poker and a pair of bellows were covered with dust. Then Michael saw a small inner door. 'What's in there?'

'Nothing,' said Artemis, 'which is why it is so sacred. There is room only for the god and you, and if you go in you have to lose yourself and find Him. If you take as much as a notebook in, you cut yourself off. And you don't kneel or pray, you simply stand and take *darshan*, which means "look". Hindus believe that if you look for long enough, something will come deep into you from what you look at. This little room is called the wombhouse because, as only God is there, with His power of life, you can, as it were, be born again.'

'Even me, an outsider?'

'There are no outsiders here.'

'Come in with me.'

'I don't go in. I have never particularly wanted to be alone with God,' and she said, 'Michael, come outside now because I must tell you why I brought you here.' Outside, sitting on the grass, she said, 'When you win your case against Cromartie, and I'm sure you will, will you use your influence and ask the Indian Government to do what Auntie Sanni and I so much want them to do, which is to let the Shiva come home here, and the temple be made fit for him?'

'I wish I could.' At that moment he truly did. 'But, darling, I have no influence.'

'I was afraid you would say that. Oh, well. It will probably be put into a museum. A pity, when you seemed to understand so well,' and she was gone, back into the courtyard where she stood, looking at the far line of sea showing in the cleft; one hand was stroking the little Nandi bull and she seemed to be struggling against tears.

Michael had followed her with determined steps. Now he took her by the shoulders and turned her to face him. 'Artemis. You didn't bring me here simply to see the temple and talk about Auntie Sanni.' He gave her a gentle shake and felt her trembling. 'There's something else, isn't there? You brought me here because?'

It came with a rush. 'I thought it was a good place to say goodbye.'

'*Goodbye!*'

'Yes, I'm leaving.'

'*Leaving?*' He was dazed.

'Yes, and I want to thank you. It has been lovely, Michael. For me it was love for the first time in my life.' Her eyes were lit to an extraordinary blue as she said, 'Perhaps the first time in yours too?'

'Yes.' He tightened his arms.

'But I have done all I had to do here.' Artemis broke away. 'Ellen understands. I have to go.'

'Go where?'

'I don't know yet. Anywhere but here.'

It sounded so forlorn that he wanted to hold her close again but he felt he had to keep to practical things.

'When?'

'Now. Today. As soon as we get back.'

'And where are you going?'

'I don't know. Anywhere. Just go.'

'You're not.' Michael took her even more firmly into his arms. 'When you leave here, you leave with me.'

'With *you*? Today?'

'If you insist.'

'I must.'

'Then there's no point in my staying here, is there?' asked Michael.

'Inspector Dutta?'

'With poor Veeranna dead?'

'Don't.' She hid her face.

'I have to. Inspector Dutta is not going to get any further. He can't find out any more from Sri Satya

Narayana. The Government will have to accept that the case must be a straightforward battle as to who gets the Shiva. I can deal with that in London better than here. Say goodbye to Nandi because we must go.'

'If only we could.'

'We can. I'll just have to see Inspector Dutta and, of course, Auntie Sanni. You pack. We'll drive to the airport – it only takes half an hour – catch the one o'clock flight to Calcutta. I'll have to drop the car off. In Calcutta, madam, I'm going to buy you a ring – an engagement ring, Artemis. We'll catch the night flight home to London and as soon as possible we'll be married and I'll never let you out of my sight again.' He stood up, 'Mahdhoo! Mahdhoo! Bring Natram. Be quick.'

Natram brought them back the way they had come and put them down on the beach, but when Michael turned towards the garden, Artemis caught his hand. 'I feel so dirty. Let's have a swim before anyone comes down.'

'Without Thambi?'

'I'll take care of you,' she teased, 'or you can stay in the shallows. We can go in just as we are – there's no one to see.' But there was. Samuel was hastening down the garden. At the same moment, Auntie Sanni appeared on the veranda, Professor Ellen beside her.

Ellen looking after her ewe lamb to the last, thought Michael, but she was not smiling, neither did Auntie Sanni wave and, as Samuel with Thambi came nearer, he saw consternation on their faces.

'Missy Sahib,' Samuel said. 'Inspector Dutta, he want to see you in his office soon as you come in. At once.'

For a moment Artemis did not move.

'Missy Sahib.'

Then Artemis dropped Michael's hand and stood clear. 'If Inspector Dutta wants me, tell him I am here in the garden,' and when Samuel had gone, 'Michael, please stay. I think I'm going to need you.'

Unusually indulgent, the Inspector came. 'Well, I wanted a full story and I thought she would tell it better here,' he told Michael. He brought his two policemen – the sergeant with his notebook. They stood at a respectful distance. 'Miss Knox, you went last night with your group to Konakpur and the Gul Mahal?'

'I didn't go with the group. Mr Dean kindly drove me.'

'I gather it is an important evening in your itinerary so it was necessary you should be there. Why did you come back?'

'I had forgotten my notes. I was to give a talk on Indian classical dancing and had to have them.'

'Is that really why?'

'I've told you. I had forgotten my notes.'

'Very convenient.'

'*In*convenient,' Artemis corrected him, 'but Mr Dean kindly came with me and drove like the wind.'

'Yet you found time to go to the village.'

'The village? Of course I didn't go to the village. Ask Mr Dean. He'll tell you. He was with me all the time.'

'All the time?'

'Yes. Weren't you, Michael?' As she looked at him her eyes held not only a plea but a challenge that said as clearly as if they had spoken, 'I thought you loved me. Well, show it. Show it now.'

'*All* the time, Mr Dean?'

The Inspector was like a hound on the scent and Michael was forced to say, 'Except when you went upstairs to get your notes.'

'Coward,' said Artemis's eyes, but aloud she said, 'I was only a few minutes.'

'How long is a few minutes? Ten? Fifteen? Twenty? Half an hour? Mr Dean?'

'Perhaps half an hour.'

'I had to check the notes through, be sure I had them all.'

'But you have just said—'

'Listen, Hem,' Michael interrupted, 'I don't know what the hell is in your mind but stop heckling. I was waiting in the car under the portico the whole time.

142

The hall was lit and I could see right into it to the stairs. If Artemis had come down before she got the notes I should have seen her.'

'Patna Hall has a back staircase,' said Inspector Dutta.

'That doesn't mean I use it.'

'No? Then if Mr Dean did not see you how is it that someone else did?'

'But there was no one about.' Always quick as mercury, Artemis realized she had betrayed herself.

'No? Shyama, I think, has no need to tell lies.'

'Shyama?'

'Remember Thambi had gone on the coach to help at the Gul Mahal with the ladies' rickshaws. You were wearing a scarlet coat and a headscarf but she knew you and was surprised to see you and, being curious, followed when you went, she says, to Veeranna's house.'

'It's her word against mine.'

'Shyama, as I think I told you, does not tell lies, and she is discreet. She did not tell anyone what she had seen until Thambi came home.'

'I can explain.'

'Good. There will have to be more than a little explanation. Can you, for instance, explain why, when you were in such a hurry, you found time to go and see Veeranna? Shyama says you were having a drink together.'

'So? Veeranna loves whisky but can only afford

143

palm-tree toddy so I often take him a bottle and we have a drink together.'

'But not, I think, *that* drink. Tell me what this was doing hidden in Veeranna's house. Isn't it part of the equipment of the film unit you brought over two years ago, a small tripod?'

'Yes, to do with the lights. They call it baby spider's legs. Oh, Veeranna, you promised you would sell it. Poor, stupid Veeranna.' Holding herself tightly, Artemis was rocking backwards and forwards in an agony of grief.

'Miss Knox,' said Inspector Dutta firmly, 'I think the time has come for you to tell me what you have been planning and doing at Patna Hall these last – it seems – three or four years, but I must warn you that everything you say will be taken down.' The sergeant, with his notebook, came nearer. 'Then I will ask you to read it through and sign it.'

'No need,' said Artemis. She was calm now. 'I won't tell *you*,' she was still scornful, 'but I want to tell Michael, Professor Ellen and Auntie Sanni, although I'm sure Auntie Sanni knows, and tell Samuel, Hannah and Thambi – all the people who matter. I should very much like to tell them. Then I should feel clean, and you,' she flung at the Inspector, 'can listen and take down anything you choose, but here in the garden. None of your offices. Michael, would you call everyone?'

When they came she said, as if she was a hostess

in her own drawing room, 'I have to begin at the beginning so this may take a long time. Wouldn't you like to sit down?' Auntie Sanni sat on the low wall that edged the lawn. The rest stood tense.

'Up to now, I have been very clever and ambitious.' Artemis's look was on Michael. 'Almost up to now, when it's too late. That's ironic, isn't it?' She gave a hard little laugh. No one else laughed.

'I was an only child, which is just as well for everyone.' She was standing facing them, wearing the orange dress she had worn last night, crumpled now. Her hair had come down, dishevelled, and she had a smudge on one cheek, but to Michael she had never seemed more beautiful. 'My father was an archaeologist, quite well known. Professor Arnold Knox.'

'Brilliant,' said Professor Ellen, 'and so good-looking. I knew him quite well but not that he had a wife and child.'

'Nor did he most of the time. You didn't know him as we knew him, my mother and I. When I think of the contrast between his life and ours, I boil with rage. He was usually away on one of his digs, making quite spectacular discoveries – I have some of that gift. He spent all he had on himself. It was Mum and her ordinary job who kept us going in our miserable little house. "He must have somewhere to go when he needs us," she used to say. He never sent any money and she, of course, never took her difficulties to the social services.'

'Why not?' asked the Inspector.

'Because she loved him. I hated him – and a child's hatred is a terrible thing – though in a way, I suppose, I too was under his spell, so I should be grateful. He did at least call me Artemis, which was outside her sphere. Hers was a very little sphere, but, oh, how faithful and forgiving. He was cruel. I expect I got that from him. Yes, I'm cruel too. I see now that she maddened him. If only, I used to think, she would round on him just once! When I was about ten, after he had hit her – oh, yes, he used to beat her up and then sit covering his eyes in remorse, he always had remorse until next time – I got a chair and hit him over the head with it as hard as I could. After that he began to show an interest, even pride, in me, but all the same I made a vow – and it wasn't a childish one – that I would never let a man be in a position where he could treat me like that, and never trust one. Until I met you, Michael. But it's better not to talk about that now.'

After a moment, she went on, 'My mother was an outstandingly pretty girl – otherwise he wouldn't have married her – and I inherited their looks. I determined, again not childishly, to make myself fit for what I meant to do. I went in for athletics, running – I won races and was particularly good at swimming. They said I was a natural – I have silver cups and shields but they were only a means to an end. Mum helped. She never let me go out to work

146

as I demanded – it had to be school, the university. Luckily I got grants – but we were always poor, going without things, hardly able to buy what we needed. All the same, she was proud of me. I got a first in archaeology, the only subject we knew anything about, yet she wanted to send me to drama school, knowing I had a secret ambition to be an actress.'

'You would have made a very good one,' said Professor Ellen bitterly.

'Oh, Ellen, I'm so sorry, I truly am. Soon, there was no question of my being an actress. My mum,' her voice quivered, 'was worn down. Being an actress was too uncertain: I had to earn a salary. But luck came my way – I believe in luck if you give it plenty of help. I gained a post. There were twenty other applicants but I got it. I used my father's name as a footstool and perhaps that helped. The post was as a research assistant in the Oriental Antiquities department of the British Museum, which I knew well. In fact, it was there that I saw my first Shiva Nataraja – they have a fine one. The keeper, Sir Richard Crewe, said he noticed me, a student, standing there gazing at it. Maybe it was that which made him take me.

'He was extraordinarily kind, taught me from his own wide knowledge, put books my way and, more importantly, believed in me. It was he who first told me I ought to go to India. I couldn't because my mother was so ill. Then she died – just when I could give her a little comfort and joy.' Again Artemis was

147

silent, biting her lip. 'One day I saw an article on Professor Ellen's tours. I showed it to Sir Richard. "It sounds the very thing," he said. "South India. That's the cradle of art. By all means go. I'll try to get you a grant," and he gave such a glowing testimonial of me to Ellen that she offered me the trip free of charge if I would act as her assistant. You see, it all began to fit in.'

'I trusted you,' said Professor Ellen.

'I know you did. Sir Richard was pleased. He said, "It will be of great help to you in your career." He didn't know that all the time I wasn't aiming at museums, no matter how prestigious, but, to me, the far more interesting and lucrative world of buying and selling. He unwittingly helped me in that way too. "I go to India whenever I can," he told me, "and send out my spies," but they looked in temples, burial grounds, far villages. They never thought of looking in Auntie Sanni's drawing room where I found the little Shiva Nataraja, alone, unprotected and accessible.'

'And I told you how valuable it was,' mourned Professor Ellen. 'God forgive me.'

'It still needed three years. I had to think how to take the statue, make its replica and, more difficult still, how to smuggle it out of India. It would have been easy to lift it, but with Ellen there, a hue and cry would have been immediate. Every way out would be watched, airports, railways, docks, ships.

There had to be another way. Anyway, I didn't waste that first trip. I hired a car and went exploring. I found quite a few small antiques – bowls and vases, an ancient cooking spoon, a ninth-century amulet that Sir Richard bought. "You do have an eye!" he said. I went to the Gul Mahal and met Natram and Mahdhoo. I learned some Telegu. I can have infinite patience when I want something badly enough, like a cat waiting for a bird. Yet I think I must have been as blind as you were, Inspector. With all my explorations I had never explored our village. Now I began to make friends here – real friends. Then, when I went to visit Veeranna, I found the solution. Like you, Michael, I saw at once what an artist he is – was,' she corrected herself, and she told the Inspector, 'Unlike you, it took Michael to see that gleam of resentment in Veeranna's eyes. Oh, Michael!'

'Never mind Michael. Go on.'

'Veeranna's father, grandfather, great-grandfather had all been potters and image-makers so it was in his blood and I guessed he could copy anything exactly, and, given the means, could do it in metal. Somehow I would find the means but I still had to go step by step. First I had to get his trust and liking.'

'And how did you do that – you who can do everything?'

'All too easily. Veeranna loved whisky but could not afford it so I got him some. He was ambitious

149

and knew he could work in metal if he were trained. I told him I would arrange it because he had been chosen by Shiva himself to do a great work. He positively shone.'

'Poor, unfortunate Veeranna.' Professor Ellen was full of pity but Artemis disregarded her.

'I still had to take it step by step but they were firm steps. I knew Sri Satya Narayana long before you heard of him. While I was at the British Museum I had written letters to him from Sir Richard and I went to see him. I had hoped he would tell me if there was a potter or sculptor in the district, but now there was Veeranna. I wrote anonymously to Sri Satya Narayana, as if from a college of art centred in Delhi, asking if he would take Veeranna – under another name, of course – as a pupil and teach him the age-old *cire perdu* method on six-week courses, three times a year, and offering what I knew was an exorbitant fee. Then I sent the money in cash and with it Veeranna, who called himself Gopal. I paid his air fares, and it all went as I planned. Veeranna told me that Sri Narayana had told him that he was the most promising pupil he had ever had. Veeranna did three courses with him before the old man died. Then he worked at home, secretly in that little room off the big one where he hid the Shiva. You will remember I was to take it to Sri Narayana for rescue treatment but I took it instead to Veeranna – just as well because Sri Narayana died.

150

'Veeranna had the Shiva for about four months, working on the copy. I provided materials, wax, clay, another kiln, tools. The villagers were so used to him drying his images in the shade that they never noticed that this one was different, and over and over again I told him that if he let out a word Shiva would punish him. I also had to manipulate you, Ellen.'

'*Me!*' Professor Ellen was indignant.

'Yes. Talk you into telling Auntie Sanni the Shiva needed treatment for salt and you got her to let me take it supposedly to Sri Narayana when I went to Kashmir for the summer and pick it up four months later and bring it home. I had calculated that that was the time Veeranna would need.

'Then I, with Auntie Sanni and the household, put the Nataraja back in its niche. Only it was not the real Nataraja. That was securely hidden behind the rafters of Veeranna's house. The niche had been made ready with flowers and lights as all the household came to worship. You know already that it was Ellen who eventually discovered the fake. What you don't know is what I had to do next.

'I had been perplexed, because when I had the Shiva how could I smuggle it out? Then I hit on the idea of the film unit, and engaged the two men to do a short film of the caves. I had worked with them before and knew that among their lighting equipment was a small cylinder made of black fibreboard that held the baby legs tripod, which would just fit the

Nataraja. Late on the night before we left, when the crew had packed and put all the equipment ready in the hall, Veeranna and I removed the baby legs – he promised he would sell them – and put the Nataraja, well wrapped in soft rags and paper, into the cylinder, sealed it and put it back, because if you want to smuggle anything through an airport, the baggage of a tour or film unit is almost always untouched, especially if there is someone there in authority. As you were, Ellen.'

'You mean *I* brought the Shiva out!' Professor Ellen sounded faint.

'You certainly did. All I had to do in New York was quietly take the cylinder and get in a taxi as fast as I could. It was clever, wasn't it?'

'You're a devil.'

'I agree. There was one thing more I had to do, perhaps more cruel than anything else. On our last night I had to take away everything I had given Veeranna for making the Nataraja – tools, materials, wax. I couldn't risk anyone finding them. I promised him I would send him money so that he could buy what he needed gradually, which would have been believable, but I shall never forget his look of agony as he helped me pack it all into the car to the last scrap of wax or shredded clay.'

'You forgot about the baby legs.'

'I didn't know about them. First thing in the morning I drove to our little sea port, hired a boat and dumped the rest of the tools far out to sea. I didn't take Veeranna with me – he might have tried to retrieve them. No one will ever find them. There, that's all.'

'By no means all.' Inspector Dutta came nearer. 'Miss Knox, I put it to you that yesterday evening you came back here from the Gul Mahal, not to fetch your notes but to visit the potter, Veeranna.'

'Of course, and to have a drink with him. As I have said before.'

'But this was a very different drink.'

'Yes.'

'Now, Miss Knox—'

But Michael could bear no more. 'Artemis. Why, oh, why, did you come back to Patna Hall? You were safely in New York.'

'Yes, but I couldn't keep away. It was like a call. You see, it wasn't finished.'

'You had the Shiva.'

'I didn't.'

'You *didn't*?' It was like a chorus.

'No. It all turned bitter, bitter. Hasn't it ever happened to you? You set your ambition on something, plan for it, work for it and when you attain it you don't want it. In New York I kept the Nataraja hidden for weeks. I dared not look at it. At last I gave it to a good needy young dealer I knew, Narayan, on condition he didn't mention me. I didn't want money, though he tried to make me take a share.

Like you, Auntie Sanni, I couldn't take money for Shiva, and Narayan sold it to Mr Cromartie.

'I thought it was finished and I could come back and it would all be the same. Instead, I found you, Inspector Dutta, and Michael. Oh, Michael. If you hadn't come with your insight, everything would have been all right, but you saw – and said you must tell Inspector Dutta. You would never have guessed on your own,' she threw at the Inspector. 'Veeranna held out against you, Michael, because he liked and trusted you, but with Inspector Dutta's "methods".' She shuddered. 'At least I saved him from that.

'Veeranna was the only one who could tell the truth. At first I thought I would tell Inspector Dutta myself. I thought that was why I had had that call. I forgot that everywhere you go you have to take yourself with you. I have never been afraid to do things, but now I was afraid of what I had done. You are quite right, Inspector, that that drink was a different one. I poisoned it and you needn't trouble yourself to find out with what, I'll tell you. It was the sap of the *kaosi* tree, quick and deadly. I should have taken it myself.'

Her eyes looked at Michael. 'You gave me a chance when you made me that wonderful offer. You don't know how wonderful it was. For a little while I let myself believe, but one mustn't tamper with the gods. It's your duty to arrest me, isn't it?'

There was silence, shock and infinite dismay.

Then Inspector Dutta spoke almost reluctantly, 'Miss Knox, theft and murder are the gravest of crimes.' Artemis had taken a few steps backwards as if she recoiled. The sergeant came closer. 'My man will have taken down everything you have said. I shall ask you to sign it. Then, yes, Miss Knox, I shall arrest you.'

'If you can.' Eluding the sergeant, she had turned and was racing to the beach, running as only Artemis could.

'After her. After her!' the Inspector screamed to his men. The younger one shot away but the sergeant stopped to lay down his notebook.

Auntie Sanni, though, had risen in anticipation, 'Thambi, come back,' and she laid her hand on Michael's arm. 'No,' she forbade him. 'It's better this way. Let her go.'

Michael shook off the hand and ran, but not to the beach, only as far as its entrance, and stopped.

Artemis was already on the high diving board, wearing the usual wicker helmet – she must have snatched it up from Thambi's row. 'She not risk to be stun.' It was Thambi's voice beside him. 'She know just what she doing, Sahib,' which, at that moment, was stripping off her dress, standing erect, naked. In the full glare of the sun she held her hands high in her pose and waited.

'She judge when the waves roll back,' Thambi whispered in admiration. 'Ah!'

The dive took her far over the panting police-men's heads, far over the surging surf. They saw the head go down, then come up again, as she swam to the protecting nets, dived under them and swam on out to sea.

'There are sharks.' Professor Ellen covered her eyes.

'Please God, no,' said Auntie Sanni.

Inspector Dutta stood furious and thwarted as Thambi, who had come back from the beach, said in defiance, 'No one catch her now. She gone.'

LONDON

'IS IT TRUE, Mrs McIndoe – or may I call you Miss Sanni?' asked Sir George Fothergill, ' – that you have never been away from Patna Hall, not even for a night?'

'Never,' said Auntie Sanni.

'Didn't you ever want to see the world? Meet people?'

'The world comes to us, Sir George. People, too, or they used to.'

When Mr Cromartie had dropped the case – he could not do anything else as the Nataraja had clearly been stolen – and gone back to Canada, the Government of India had decided that it would be only fair to offer it back to Auntie Sanni as Henry Bertram's granddaughter. 'We will build you a temple.'

'Please no,' said Auntie Sanni. 'We could not use a temple.' Nor would she take a penny. 'A gift is a gift,' she said. 'I only ask that it stays in this country where it belongs. There is a little temple in the hills . . .'

The Government had still brought her over to London. 'We need you as we must have an official declaration of your wonderful gift of the Nataraja to India. Mr Bhatacharya and our London lawyers will see to that, and they are arranging for you to meet all the experts at a celebratory reception in your honour.' To Michael's surprise she had accepted, though nothing would stir the Colonel. She had had an official escort on the plane but Michael had been deputed to meet her and take her to stay with Honor Wyatt.

Auntie Sanni had made few concessions for London and still wore her Mother Hubbards, but she had shoes instead of sandals and was wrapped in a large *paschmina* shawl, its fine pure wool intricately embroidered.

'Auntie Sanni,' Michael had asked her, 'is there anything you would particularly like to do or see in these three days?' She would not stay any longer.

'Shops?' suggested Honor.

'I never shop.'

'Would you come and visit my museum?' That was Sir Richard Crewe.

'Thank you, but no museums.'

'A visit to the Houses of Parliament and lunch on the terrace?' asked Mr Bhatacharya. 'The foreign secretary would be delighted.'

'No, thank you.'

'The Tower and the Crown Jewels?'

'I know jewels.'

'Then what?'

'Ordinary things. I should like to take a day just to see this city, if Michael would come with me. I suppose it would have to be by car – it is too big to walk. I should like to drive all round it, not to beauty spots or sights but everyday streets, homes, parks and especially the Thames.'

'Why the Thames?'

'It flows out to sea. That will bring me back to scale and I can go back refreshed.'

'And you can really stay only three days?'

'That is enough. Besides I have much to do at home. We are closing Patna Hall, Sir George. It has had its time.'

'Sad,' said Sir George. 'I was hoping I could come and stay with you.'

'We shall still have spare rooms for our friends and we shall still be there, the Colonel and I, Samuel our faithful butler and his wife Hannah, our house-keeper. Thambi, our lifeguard, will stay in his lodge but we shall demolish most of the main house. The sale of the land will pay for it.'

'This is where we should help,' said Mr Bhata-charya. 'At least let us give something towards the cost.'

'I can take no money for Shiva-ji.'

Honor had drawn Michael away. 'This must be very painful for you.' Michael had told her every-thing. 'Poor Michael, you look five years older.'

'But I feel richer not poorer. I had her.'

'And will have, for ever.'

'To the end of my life,' said Michael. 'Artemis.'

———

Mr Bhatacharya was still trying to persuade Auntie Sanni. 'After all, you and your grandfather sheltered the Nataraja and let him be worshipped for close on a hundred years.'

'That is why I can take nothing for him.' Then Auntie Sanni stopped. 'There is one thing I should like you to do.'

'Of course. No matter what.'

'That first offer you made to the man Cromartie. Michael told me about it. Wasn't it fifty thousand pounds?'

'Yes, and at first he thought it generous.'

'Please make it to him again – pounds not dollars.' Auntie Sanni smiled – Walter had told her the whole story of his meeting with Mr Cromartie. 'Fifty thousand pounds – not dollars. After all, he did bring the Nataraja home.'

AFTERWORD

This book is a twin; more than that, a Siamese twin, in that places, people, even phrases are taken from another of my books.

A few years ago I wrote a novel, *Coromandel Sea Change*, set in an old-fashioned hotel, Patna Hall, on South India's Coromandel coast. The sub-continent of India is shaped like a vast pear-drop and this is on its eastern side.

When the novel was half-way through, my attention was caught by a newspaper article in *The Times* of such interest to me that I immediately became aware that I had two plots for the same novel, something most uncommon and inconvenient because they were both so strong that I could not blend them. I had to choose and so went back to my original one which, I am glad to say, met with a measure of success.

In 1994 I had to spend some time in India to make the BBC's documentary programme *Bookmark* which, in the course of its journeyings, took me back to that eastern coast again. Perhaps it was this that made my second plot erupt into life.

As I have said, the book is based on truth – as can be seen by the newspaper cutting that first caught my eye.

Museums fear for their treasures
Bronze idol must be returned to Hindu temple

By Andrew Billen

A High Court decision to return to India a twelfth century bronze idol worth more than £250,000 may have put under threat other art treasures in the possession of British collectors and museums.

Mr Justice Kennedy ruled that the Nataraja, a statue of the Hindu god Siva, belonged to a ruined temple in Tamil Nadu and said that similar ownership claims could be made.

'Many will fail but some will succeed, particularly if the criminal character of their taking could be proved,' he said. The judgement ends a legal battle that began in August 1982 when Scotland Yard seized the Nataraja as it was being examined in the British Museum.

The Nataraja had lain buried in the temple grounds for centuries when it was dug up in 1976 by a labourer while he was building a cowshed. He sold it for 200 rupees (£12).

By 1982, it had come into the ownership of a London antiques dealer who sold it for £50,000 to the Bumper Development Corporation, a Canadian company controlled by Mr Robert Bordon, an oil magnate, art collector and philanthropist.

It had been handed to a conservator at the British Museum for advice on its transportation to Canada when police intervened.

The judge ruled that while Mr Bordon's behaviour could not be faulted, the labourer from India, Mr S. Ramamoorthi, was guilty of criminal misappropriation under local law.

The case was complicated by some recondite issues, in-

164

cluding whether a consecrated deity such as the Nataraja can be regarded as property. The Indians who wanted its return claimed its divine properties did not prevent its remaining a lump of stone.

The judge also had to decide which of the co-plaintiffs was the rightful owner. Rejecting the claims of the Union of India, the local state, a public official of the Temple and Siva Lingham, a cylindrical piece of stone representing a Hindu god, he decided the ruined temple itself was a legal entity capable of suing.

He said: 'I am satisfied that the pious intention of the twelfth century notable who gave the land and built the Pathur temple, remains in being and is personified by the temple itself, a juristic entity.'

Yesterday, a spokesman for the Indian High Commission applauded the ruling. He said: 'The judgement is very welcome encouragement for us. As a result we may be able to open the way for others of our things to come back to us.'

Both the Victoria and Albert Museum, which has a collection of 33,000 Indian paintings, sculptures and textiles, and the British Museum, which owns hundreds of religious objects from India and Asia, have followed the case keenly.

The two museums said yesterday that they did not believe that any of their exhibits were in immediate danger, but that they would need to examine the judgement in detail.

The Times,
20 February 1988

Through an experienced researcher, I managed to collect several other articles and then, by tremendous luck, was lent the documentary book of the trial, which opens with an account of a writ issued by a Canadian antique dealer against the State of Tamil Nadu in India for the return of an eleventh-century Nataraja, which he had brought to London to sell and which had been impounded by the British police.

The Union of India & Others v Bumper Development Corporation Judgement

INTRODUCTION

0.1 The issue which I have tried arises in an action brought by Bumper Corporation Ltd ('Bumper') against the Commissioner of the Metropolitan Police and two of his officers to recover an antique Indian bronze sculpture. The Police interpleaded between Bumper and the State of Tamil Nadu, who had asserted a claim to the bronze. On 10 February, 1983, by consent, Master Waldman ordered that the following question and issue should be tried:

> 'Whether the State of Tamil Nadu can prove that it has a title to the Bronze which is superior to the title of the Bumper Development Corporation to the Bronze, and that meantime all further proceedings in this action relating to such other questions or issues be stayed until the trial of the said preliminary issues or until further order.'

This account of the trial goes on for 145 closely typed pages and is unutterably tedious, confusing and complicated; so many claimants followed Bumper that the Government of India launched a counter-claim in which the god Shiva became the plaintiff.

I decided finally to keep to the Judge's opening – its first two paragraphs – and let my story be almost completely imaginary.

APPENDIX

SHIVA NATARAJA

Shiva Nataraja – S. India AD 1100. Shiva manifests five aspects of eternal energy: creation, preservation, destruction, concealment, favour. He is seen here as Supreme God and Lord of the Dance. In his upper right hand he holds a drum representing the primordial sound of creation. The upper left hand holds a flame of destruction: indicating the overcoming of opposites in the nature of this great god echoed by wearing both female and male ear-rings. He makes the gesture 'have no fear' and points to his raised left foot, symbolising release. He treads upon the prostrate dwarf of ignorance, 'Apasmara', and the diminutive figure of the Goddess Ganga appears in his flowing hair. The God maintains an exquisite poise and equanimity at the centre of the whirling cycle of cosmic activity.

Plaque from the glass case holding the great Nataraja in the Department of Oriental Antiquities in the British Museum.

By permission of the Keeper, Robert Knox.

ACKNOWLEDGEMENTS

I should like to give my most sincere thanks to those experts who have so generously helped me with the plot and writing of this book, extraordinarily difficult and intricate as it was.

To Mr and Mrs Talbot, Rina and Rupert of New Delhi, and their colleague Mr Reddy of southern India, for their constant advice on location and custom.

To Robert Knox, Keeper of the Department of Oriental Antiquities at the British Museum, London, who, by happy coincidence, was one of the experts called in by the Government of India to identify the dancing Shiva. He not only taught me a great deal and gave valuable advice but actually lent me his book containing an account of the statue and trial *and* let me keep it until my writing was done.

To Andrew Henley, barrister, for his long and patient help on matters of law, and his wife Kris who acted as a 'go-between'. Also Fraser Barber, film sound recordist, for many practical suggestions. To my brilliant editor at Macmillan Publishers, Hazel Orme, and friend and typist Sheila Anderson, whose patience never seems to wear out.

169

And to my long-suffering family and staff. Once someone asked my elder daughter Jane if she too wanted to be a writer when she grew up. 'No thank you,' was the candid answer. 'One in the family is enough.'

R.G.
1997